those who lie will fade and die

Peter Raposo

APS Books
Yorkshire

APS Books,
The Stables Field Lane, Aberford, West Yorkshire, LS25 3AE

APS Books is a subsidiary of the
APS Publications imprint

www.andrewsparke.com

First published worldwide by APS Books in 2023

For my mother

♥

an outer dimensional breakup story

"Once you give up everything, everything makes sense."

M÷

Coventry, May 2023

Prologue

Both the lockdown of 2020 and the end of my marriage also in the same year were lessons I needed to learn, trials that I had to endure so I could become a bit colder and wiser, especially when it comes to loving and giving. They were harsh lessons that would send me on a journey which would take years, a journey through the Dark Night of the Soul but it was actually a journey of self-discovery, and along the way I met a diverse variety of characters/people that I would have never met had I stayed trapped in that loveless marriage of mine. Some things are meant to happen and afterwards the writer must write about it and leave behind some sort of testimony, a testimony where he or she is the hero/heroine (or anti-hero/heroine) of a real-life tale, and while we make our journey through this book called Life we must evolve both as human beings and spiritual beings, learn the lessons that we are meant to learn, learn and evolve, change for the better, and we must even forgive those who have somehow hurt us and sent us towards that journey which we had to take but which we weren't even aware of, and after forgiving them, sadly as this may sound, no matter how much we used to love them, sometimes, after doing our inner child healing, we have to leave some of those people behind - maybe not forever; maybe we will see them again in the near future, or in a distant future - but while we're healing and evolving we can't be near those who have hurt us, or, if they live nearby, we must somehow find a way of avoiding them for a long time.

Browsing through recent notes I found myself travelling back in time, metaphorically speaking of course (I'm not Chance the Time Traveller; more about him later on), to a time where I wanted to write the type of book I'm writing right now but the circumstances (and my laziness) didn't allow me to write. Instead of writing I would spend my time and money going from place to place in search of the same things that I'm searching right now (and some of which I already have), but back then I was really lost and I didn't even know what I was searching for. To say that I was lost is actually an understatement.

I was wasting sperm on others, sperm and saliva and words and money, going to places I wish never to return to, meeting people I wish never to see again, but I was so lonely and lost that I would look for company anywhere. And at the same time I was looking for God, for salvation, praying almost every day, but how can a person find salvation (and God) if we spend our lives lost in the darkness? Now I finally understand that a lot of the time we need isolation so that we can work on ourselves and on our dreams, but it took me decades and a bit of self-therapy for me to finally come to terms with loneliness and isolation.

In 1999 I found myself in a cinema seat with a bag of popcorn and a large Pepsi in front of me, and even though the cinema wasn't that full I sat close to a lonely woman, only three seats away from her. We were sitting right at the back, middle seats, no one else on the next row of seats.

The movie we were watching was *Eyes Wide Shut*, a film directed by Stanley Kubrick, a director whose movies I both adore (Paths of Glory, Spartacus, The Shining, 2001: A Space Odyssey – one of my favourite movies of all time) and don't (A Clockwork Orange, Barry Lyndon). It's a movie that would be the last film directed by Mr Kubrick as he would die, aged 70, six days after showing the final cut to Warner Brothers. Throughout the years people have written all sort of rumours about that same movie, going as far as saying that Mr Kubrick was killed because he knew and was about to show too much to the audience. Some people even went as far as saying that Mr Kubrick was sharing some of the Invisible Hand's rituals with the world; the sacrifices that the Invisible Hand makes to their fake god.

On that evening I didn't see the entire movie. Something happened during the movie, something that, looking back now, was kind of funny and also super-scary.

Eyes Wide Shut is a long movie, and sometime during the movie the woman that was sitting only a few seats away from me made a soft groaning noise, and when I turned around to look at her I saw that she was touching herself and that her panties were down, around her knees. I saw the darkness and saw her looking at me, eye to eye, daring me to join her. A few seconds passed and she leaned against the seat, still looking at me, pleasing herself, daring me to join her, and because I was lost, so damn lost, I slowly stood up and was about to join her, but just then I felt something grab my left arm, strongly pulling me away from the woman, and I thought that one of the cinema workers had seen us and was about to tell me off and throw us both out of the cinema, but when I turned around I saw no one around me - not a soul, nothing but darkness. I stood there for I don't know how long just looking at the darkness, looking but seeing nothing. The thought of joining that woman was suddenly dissolved. Instead, I made my way out of the cinema, almost running as I left the woman behind, and later, when I found myself alone in a park, I burst into tears. Looking back now, I don't even know what happened on that night, but whatever it was it was probably a blessing.

÷

Life's a journey, a crazy journey with good moments and bad moments in between. No one knows where they're going. Sometimes I feel as if we're characters in a game. No one knows what the final destination will be, what's beyond the Veil. Actually, now that I think about it, some people do know what's beyond the Veil but they're sworn to secrecy and they can only share that knowledge with members of their tribe. Without us even being aware of it, as we go through life, we're split into different tribes, and sometimes we leave one tribe and join another, and secrets are shared with us, secrets that aren't really secrets, secrets that are actually teachings, teachings that have been passed orally and even through scriptures throughout the ages, but because some people can't understand those teachings, or maybe it requires too much from them, those same people then leave their tribe and join either another tribe or become independent souls in a world where you need other souls with you. Or they get lost to the sins of the flesh and decide to stay in the world of fornication and drugs, unaware that, when they do that, they will never cross the Veil.

The darkness is real. Sometimes strong men and strong women get lost in it, perish in it, and later their souls will never cross the Veil. But will they be given another chance? Resurrection blues? I don't know.

We're the lost children of Eve walking in the darkness, lost in the wilderness, but if we stop for a little while and listen, stop and disconnect from the online world and connect to Nature, we might be able to hear a voice, a Voice in the Wilderness, a Voice guiding us away from the darkness.

I came to The Bear and Ragged Staff pub in Bedworth for something to eat, and I sat right at the back, Table 5. Looking to my left, I found two books by an author called Marie Corelli. I had never heard of the author before. The books were *The Life Everlasting* and *The Mighty Atom*, both hardback copies, pages yellowed with the passage of time. I reached for *The Life Everlasting*, opened it, and read the author's prologue. And as my eyes were going down the lines of that book I felt not only as if I was reading something written for me but also written by me. In the first sentence of her prologue Marie mentions the Voice, my Voice, the Voice I heard in 2021, a 'Voice in the Wilderness'. That only shows me that we're all connected and we don't even know it.

The date: 11th January 2023. I've just discovered the works of Marie Corelli.

I came to Bedworth for a meal only because I had to go to George Eliot Hospital to collect some medication, and on the way back to Coventry I decided to stop in Bedworth and get something to eat. I almost went to the City Arms in Earlsdon for a meal but I want to disappear for a while and avoid certain areas at certain times.

My new novel had just been completed and while I was making my way to the hospital I wrote the lyrics for a song with the same title as my new novel. They're both called *cast away your dreams of darkness*. They talk about lost love, about the Light, the Light of God, the Light inside us, and how we must believe again in the power of love.

I love someone but I lost her, and now I must retreat for a while, ponder about stuff, pray and wait. I almost went back to dating again but my heart wasn't yet ready for it. How could I love someone so quickly after losing the woman I love?

There was a bit of bitterness inside me, a bit of coldness, and it wouldn't be fair for me to start dating and then give the worst version of myself to someone else. And so now I must retreat and wait. And while I'm waiting I must heal and erase that bit of bitterness that I have inside myself.

Cast away your dreams of darkness
Cast away your dreams of darkness,
Believe again in the power of love.
Gather the pieces of your broken heart

And run towards the light.
The light
The light
Delight
The light is inside of you
It was diminished by heartbreak
But faith will show you the way
And enlighten your path.

We're children, lost in the Matrix
Children in a simulation game.
We must get away from our screens
And connect to nature, connect to the light.

Get away from the darkness and connect to the light.

The Son said, "Unless you change and become like little children, you will never enter the kingdom of heaven."
Unless you change and see the light, you will forever be lost in the darkness.

Cast away your dreams of darkness,
Believe again in the power of love.
Gather the pieces of your broken heart
And run towards the light.
The light
The light
Delight
The light is love.
The light is good.
The light is God.

get away from the darkness~

The darkness isn't you.
You're not the darkness.

I found out that by staying away from sin I also manage to stay away from the darkness. A bad thought might try to set me off track, but if I push myself forward and concentrate on the Lord, I always manage to get away from the darkness. I wrote the lyrics for *cast away your dreams of darkness* while walking past the All Saints churchyard in

Chilvers Coton. A bad thought came to my head and I was quick to shake it away and told myself, "Go to God. Now! Sing a song to Him."

And then I sang the first lines of the song, "Cast away your dreams of darkness, Believe again in the power of love."

I sang to myself only, to myself and to God because I didn't want to fall back into the darkness.

The darkness is everywhere, even inside ourselves, but, as I've often said, we're not the darkness. We're light.

We're the light of heaven, the light of the Creator.

Stay clean, keep the faith, and when you cross the Veil the light will guide you and the love will find you. This is what is taught amongst other tribes, and I'm sharing some of the secrets with you: Believe again in the power of Love (God) and you will find the light. The Light is inside us.

I look at what I wrote; yesterday, the year before, and the year before that...and...and I see a new me, the same but different, slightly changing, leaving certain things behind.

It is a cold afternoon. Soon I will get changed, drive to church, pray the Rosary, and then it's the same old scenario as the previous years, the same but different. Certain things will remain the same but certain things have changed. A change was needed and so I changed. And I'm still changing.

Jeff Beck has died.

Lisa Marie Presley has died.

Little by little the names of your past disappear.

One day it will be your turn to disappear, but where will you go once the journey of the body comes to an end?

A cold afternoon but the sun is shining so bright. I look at the time. Time to get changed, time to do so much and so little at the same time. Time to move on but where can I go?

In a healthy relationship you don't ask what's going on, you don't cry, and you certainly don't wonder where you are.

And so the bitch rode on her unicorn towards hell; I wanted to start a story like this. It would be a crazy story about a love that wasn't there. It would be an outer dimensional love story. Make that an outer dimensional breakup story. Should I write that story?

Why not?

Read on.

Sadly there are no unicorns but hell is real.

10th January 2023

Even though they had a few disagreements in the past, Logan Paul seems to be backing one of Andrew Tate's theories by tweeting, 'The Matrix is real and you better pray you never become one of its targets.'

Is Logan referring to the Invisible Hand?

Should I even be writing this?

According to something that Tate has said, the Matrix is a force controlled by the media, governments and big corporations. Those three combined lead to the mysterious Invisible Hand. And talking about the Matrix, how come no one is talking about the Biden files but everyone was quick to go after Trump's files? The people see it and at the same time they are blind to it.

The sheep walk in the darkness, their faces glued to their mobile phones and to the Lie, but while they are walking in the darkness they forget that there is a light inside them that can lead them to greater things, one of those things being the Truth. But they just won't switch off from the Lie and connect to the Truth.

I've gone missing from certain places, missing from the lives of certain people. It's okay. I needed to get away from them, avoid certain places. If you're not missed, go somewhere where someone wants you. Search for that place, for people who want to be with you. Search for the light and avoid the darkness.

The darkness doesn't need company and you for sure don't need the loneliness in your life.

I'm getting good at becoming a ghost. I had a good teacher.

A poet that I know sits alone at the City Arms reading Immanuel Kant. The moment she sees me she calls out for me. She's eager to share Kant's ideas with me but I just want to be left alone.

"I'm okay," I say to her when she asks how I am and I don't stop. I move along, towards another room, a quiet corner at the pub, a place where no one can see me. I sit with my back towards everyone, head down, a notebook in front of me. I'm slowly retreating, becoming a ghost.

Days go by when I don't even check my mobile phone.

Messages remain unread, but not that many, and not for too long.

In the past I said too much, shared too much, was always visible, but that didn't work so I've decided to change.

Even my tastes have changed, or I forced myself to change. But I'm okay with the changes. For lunch I have a plant wrap instead of a duck wrap, and afterwards I have a decaffeinated Americano instead of a strong cup of coffee. Another day, a change here and there.

Where you when I needed you?

The flame is extinguished, or is it your love? And did you ever love me? Did you ever love? Truly love?

Can you love?

Or is it just me who you can't love?

The flame is extinguished, or is it the love?

I feel for those who have never truly loved. Then again, maybe they're the lucky ones. No love, no pain, but is that a good way of living? It can't be. Imagine living without love? No wonder some people are truly lost.

I have learned how to become a ghost, one with the night, one with nothingness. The indifference led me there. The indifference and coldness of others led me there. Bit by bit I'm coming out of the darkness. I am almost whole. Love damaged me. Maybe being in love isn't the right thing to do. Don't fall in love. Wait for someone else to fall in love with you. And then love them back. If someone doesn't love you and doesn't appreciate your goodness and love, walk away. Don't waste your time on nothing. Nothing leads to nothing. Who the hell would want nothing?

Ellie…

Ellie wants nothing.

Some names will hardly be mentioned, not unless they change, or I might mention them briefly, here and there, on these lines, scroll down, or quit right now. After all, every once in a while even the past needs to be revisited so you won't commit the same mistakes. Even loving someone so fast, too quickly, can be a huge mistake. Yes, even love can be a mistake, one of gigantic proportions. Revisit the past, if you must, and learn from it.

The lost children of Eve lost, just waiting to confess our sins. This morning I sit still. Nothing to confess? Hmm, there's always something to confess, but this morning, after Mass, I remain on my seat. I pray, and while I'm praying I allow myself to be loved.

God loves us while we're praying.

God loves us all the time, even (especially?) when we're lost.

My friend Edith goes to confession. She's over sixty. Everyone sins, no matter our age, no matter how good we are.

I'm getting good at avoiding sin. I must say that ever since I've started to pray the Rosary I sin less. Days go by where I'm at my cleanest; no sin at all. Let's hope I stay this way.

After prayers I stay at church for a bit longer. A few friends have been made. A few more are made.

In the house of God I allow myself to be loved. (But isn't the world the house of God?)

Aren't we the House of God?

For a long time I thought of myself as being unworthy of love but now I know better. And I loved the wrong people. Or maybe I loved too much at the wrong time. Then again, when I think about it, I come to the conclusion that those I loved didn't love me. They were simply looking for a solution for their problems, a friend to kill the loneliness, a piece of meat to satisfy the flesh. I took that role, the role of the rejected lover, the role of the failed poet (but, little by little, I'm making it as an author), a painful role to play, but pain is a lesson, and once the lesson is over you walk away and take the pain with you. But don't let the pain become your whole self. Sooner or later you have to heal. And don't wait to move on only after you're healed. That can take a long time. Instead move on while you're still healing. One day you will look behind and laugh at the absurdity of it all. You will look at someone you once loved and think to yourself, 'What was I thinking?'

Trust me, it will happen. But some faces do stay with us forever, as a reminder of what once was, a reminder of lost love, but if you loved and they didn't love you back, the loss is theirs, not yours.

It took me a long time to heal.

I should have known better but…

…but…

Now I love cautiously. Thank God I haven't forgotten how to love.

The poetess leaves Kant behind and comes over to where I am, to say hello, to see what's happening, maybe to see why I have gone cold, but she's wrong; I haven't gone cold. Or indifferent. I'm only protecting myself against the indifference of others. Not so long ago I loved too much, I loved without protection, and by that I don't mean to say that I loved without a condom (but I did that too, which was okay, as we were only seeing each other). What I meant to say is I jumped into a relationship without thinking, and then I gave too much too soon, and found myself waiting on nothing. Now I can slightly laugh about it, but for a long time I felt the breakup, and it hurt like hell. But life goes on, and I healed while moving. As a matter of fact, I'm still healing. And I still love her, just a tiny bit. I'm not that cold yet. But I will forget.

The poet taps me on the shoulder and then asks, "What's up? What's going on? Where have you been?"

Too many questions in one single go.

I came here to rest, to hide, and to write, and not to answer question after question.

I shrug my shoulders. I have nothing to say. And then I raise an eyebrow. Nothing at all (to say).

I swam in the dark and God showed me the light. How can I explain this to the poet? She's an atheist.

A mad man enters the pub. I see him here quite often. A few times he's sworn at me for no reason whatsoever. The third time he swore at me I swore back at him. Now he leaves me alone. Sometimes, when someone steps on your foot, you also have to step on them. That's how they learn their lesson and leave you alone.

Not only is the poet an atheist, she's also bisexual. And a refugee. But I don't care. I used to care about certain labels but now I see that we are all the same. A bit different but still the same.

When she sees that I'm not saying much, the poet starts talking about literature. She knows that I like Bret Easton Ellis and she tells me he has a new novel coming out this month called *The Shards*. I didn't know that. It's good to know that Bret is writing fiction again. I quickly write the name of his book down. Afterwards the poet leaves me alone. Before returning to her table, the poet says, "I wrote a new poem. And a short story. I wanted for you to read them both. Some other time, maybe?"

Some other time, maybe.

Maybe never.

Some other time, in a previous life, I would have wasted my time, nod and comply, and do something I didn't want to, but you learn your lessons as you go through life. You must learn your lessons.

Once more, I sit alone, my back to the world, the notebook waiting for notes. I write for less than one hour before getting a refill of hot chocolate. The poet is still reading Kant. She sees me and smiles. I nod before retreating back to my seat. Yes, the old me is definitely on a break.

Peter 1:23 comes to mind while I'm writing. Maybe I have been born again, too.

The Pepsi Drinker is at the pub and so is the Gambler.

The Pepsi Drinker always orders two glasses of Pepsi and then sits alone glued to his mobile phone. He seems to be a quiet person, a bit of a dreamer. As for the Gambler, she always looks a mess. And she's putting on weight. I don't know what she does but she always seems to have money to waste on the fruit machines and alcohol. She wastes a fortune on the slot machines, a bit like my friend Cassio who's also addicted to gambling. But Cassio is getting better, gambling less.

I resume my writing.

Later, when I'm about to leave, I quickly say goodbye to the poet and see that she's reading a collection of poems by Rumi. The poet reading the poet.

I tell her about Joshua Jennifer Espinoza, a poet I read recently, and also about the poetry of Roberto Bolaño.

"I've read Bolaño's poetry," she says. "Some of it I like. Others not so much. I also read *Last Evenings On Earth* not so long ago. I loved that book. Loved every single story in that book."

I'm relapsing.

I've already said too much.

Of course, I'm not really going cold, cold; cold to the point of becoming indifferent, but the years of 2019, 2020, 2021, and 2022 were a lesson, harsh slaps on my face, so I've decided to become a bit distant. But I also met a lot of good souls during that time, and I managed to get a lot of my books published, so I can't really complain.

Love came into my life in 2021, and it stayed with me for over a year, but what I called love turned out to be a disappointment, and instead of learning my lesson, I kept returning to the disappointment. What happened was I had blinds over my eyes and I was feeling a bit weak, a bit needy, and I couldn't see what was in front of me. She wasn't a bad woman. She just wasn't there. After a while she let me go, but I still pursued her, for a few months, until one day I saw that I was pursuing nothing, no one. I had a dream. She could have been part of that dream but she chose not to be, and after a while I really had to forget her and move on. But it's okay to move on. It is necessary to move on. It is a need.

If you stop (living) for someone else, if you get lost in grief or even anger, you're not doing yourself any favours. Chasing after someone who doesn't want you in their lives is a waste of time, and time is precious. If they want to go, let them go. Better yet, kick them out of your lives.

I retreat.

The Ego has accepted the Loss.

Choose yourself and you will find someone who will choose you.

A few days later, I'm back at the pub, just a few minutes after 11am, and I order breakfast and a cup of coffee. I sit at Table 29, open a notebook, and write. A few minutes later, the Gambler arrives. She goes straight to the fruit machines. The disease is calling out for her. Her addiction is the disease. And would you believe me if I said that the Pepsi Drinker arrives a few minutes after the Gambler's arrival? Two Pepsis on the table, he goes straight to his mobile phone. The same old faces almost every week, sometimes almost every day, but I like it here.

A few days ago I was in here with my friend, Jason, another local author, and we spoke about life, literature, love, and, like me, Jason is happy to stay in this city forever and do as little travelling as possible. I've lived in a few countries, made love to a few women, written stories in Portugal, France, Spain, and England, and now I want to sit still; find my own home and sit still, travel as little as possible, and love one woman only.

She was part of my dream but she chose to walk away.

Now I must find someone else to share my dream with.

The wicked say, "There is no God."

Poor souls.

Poor souls indeed because they live a godless life.

God has guided me towards a state of stillness, towards calmness of the mind and the soul.

When I'm with God, everything seems to run along better, but when I fall into temptation, life always gets a bit worse.

Psalm 14:1

In Psalm 11:5, I read, *The LORD tests the righteous and the wicked…*

Right now, in case you haven't noticed it (let go of the phone!!!), the world (all of us) are being tested, and I see so many people lost to wickedness.

I read somewhere that Bethel's original name was Luz.

Luz means light.

God is Light.

Last night I dreamt of her. I thought I was forgetting her but there she was, in my dreams. I run my hand along her back, felt the bones on her back, her flat stomach pressed against my chubby stomach. We were in bed, feeling one another, loving silently and even telepathically, loving with feeling, which sometimes I felt was something that was missing from our relationship. And now she's gone, slowly becoming a stranger, a memory, but every once in a while she still visits me in my dreams. One day there will be no dreams and her face will become a blur. Unless…

I tried to analyse the dream, see what it meant, but maybe it meant nothing and a part of me still misses her even though I'm trying to forget her. Some people believe that dreaming of a past love (but she is a recent love, still fresh on my mind) may be us recalling a past trauma in a relationship, or maybe you're unsettled with the way things ended between the two of you and you're looking for some sort of closure, but me dreaming about her probably means nothing.

Do I still miss her?

Sometimes yes.

Sometimes no.

Most of the times, yes, but when I relive the relationship I get a bit angry at the way the two of us behaved. While I was the needy one in the relationship, she was the cold one, at times even indifferent. But when she loved, she truly loved, and I miss that hidden person of hers (and that beautiful smile), the one who could love, but because she was scared of loving (or maybe she didn't love me at all) and of being hurt, she retreated, and then hurt me. Looking back, I come to the conclusion that maybe she never loved me, or maybe what she

15

felt for me wasn't enough for her to stay in a relationship with me. But that's all in the past now, and there's nothing I can do about it. Instead of letting it upset me I swallow my pride, a bit of anger, even my ego, and start again.

After a breakup, starting again is all the dumpee can do. Some people will disagree with me, and that's fine; we can all disagree about stuff and still remain respectful towards one another, and those who disagree (with me) will say that instead of moving on the dumpee can cry, which many of us do when we lose someone we love, and that the dumpee can go into no-contact mode, for months if needed, even years (!!!!!!), and wait for the dumper to see the light and return, but that might never happen and the dumpee will never be able to get those months back. I'll be honest and admit that I waited on Ellie, and after the breakup, I even pursued her, but then I saw that I was being a fool and that I was acting needy and weak, which wasn't a good look. Sadly, or luckily, after a while I got sick of it all, even sick of the love I felt for her, and instead of pursuing or waiting, I chose to walk away and move on with my life. And instead of crying about it, I accepted the heartbreak, took it as a lesson, and then, finally, I moved on. And I did cry a bit. It's okay to cry but it's not okay to drown in tears.

÷

Some humans have some sort of superpower. It's true. They're not witches or wizards or whatever. They can predict the future, they possess second sight. Ages ago someone told me bits of my future. She was right about everything. And more than once, second sight or premonition warned me of something that was about to happen, so when it came my way I was already prepared for it and armed with a solution.

÷

Those were the days, or so I thought (but the lust blinded me), when you came into my life, the light after the darkness, or a dimmed light in the dark. I gave you everything and got nothing in return, or close to nothing, but that's the way life works and we must learn from our mistakes.

I go through some old notes and type it all down. I need to remember so I won't repeat it.

I wrote bits on loose sheets of paper, Post-it notes, and even on napkins, and now I'm writing some of it down. A lot of those notes will stay undated, the people unnamed. Take a guess, I say, see which one you are, heartbreaker.

I'm getting tired of it all, even tired of some people. Bloody hell, what do people want? If you're too nice, you're too nice. If you're mean, you're mean.

I fell in love with the best part of her, before I saw the coldness, the indifference.

I am living but sometimes I'm dying.

I read about the past and I can't help smiling about it. For a long time I was haunted by the neediness, by the need to be loved. Now I'm tired of it all, even tired of the needy me. That's actually good news.

Hypatia: "Reserve your right to think, for even to think wrongly is better than not to think at all."

÷

What's happening with Andrew Tate? There isn't a lot about him on the news. Is he trapped in the Matrix?

The Matrix is controlled by the Invisible Hand.

The Invisible Hand controls (almost) everything.

Go against it and you'll be in big trouble.

A lot of influencers want the fame and the big bucks, unaware that to achieve those things they must go down the rabbit hole, and then go down on someone else and keep quiet about it. Epstein was a puppet of the Invisible Hand and look at what happened to him. And then there were the victims and the abusers and the visitors to Epstein's island, and we still don't know much about it even though Ghislaine was arrested. The monsters have been in power for a long time and the monstrosity keeps on growing, taking over (almost) everything, and that includes what children will be taught from day one. Only the Light can save us but some people are walking in the Dark. They love the darkness (and the monstrosity), and they want for the world to follow their path. The Son told us to go through the Narrow Gate but the majority of the people are running towards the Gates of Hell – and one of the main bad guys is called Gates.

Niko, a blogger-writer from Ohio, is saying that more and more people are waking up to the truth. Only a fool (and there are so many out there) would believe that there's nothing wrong with the world today.

The reptilians are enslaving the world through technology and through the lies they spread online, through music, media, etc., but a lot of people can't see it, Niko writes.

Reptilians?

Orwell and Huxley warned us of the dangers to come. They did this by writing science-fiction novels. I'm trying to do the same but some people don't want to know the truth. They've been blinded by the pleasures of this world and have forgotten about the World to Come.

St. Thérèse of Lisieux, Little Way

-a person can learn so much from the past, from the words and works of others.

Saints and holy people still walk amongst us but we hardly ever hear about them. God has been taken out of most schools and the ones in power are replacing Him with their own Agenda. A scary world we live in.

Niko says that Schwab and his pals and the WFE are trying to take over the world and control everything, even farming, and no one will be able to stop them. Powerful politicians and other so-called powerful people won't say a word about it because they were at Epstein's island, had sex with minors, everything was recorded, and now they have to keep their mouths shut. It's either that or prison.

And how old is DiCaprio's new girlfriend? Old enough to be his daughter...and beyond.

And these same people that are trying to sell you the Climate Agenda are travelling the world on their private jets. Can't you see that they want to enslave us?

÷

Some people are broken and they can't love.

I am broken, too, but I can still love. And I'm trying to heal myself, from within.

When someone leaves you, or when someone betrays you, don't ever think you're the one to blame for it. The problem is some people fall easily into temptation while others are too afraid to commit. Don't follow their path or their example.

When it came to love I was never that greedy. Whenever I was in a relationship I always remained faithful. My father's behaviour towards my mother (and other women) made me see that I didn't want to live the type of life he lived. I wasn't always an angel, but with age, and with the Word as guidance, I saw that I wanted to live a clean life, sort of a monk's life, a life of devotion and giving, a life of mediation and prayer. I'm not there yet but I'm working on it.

The world we live in is now something straight out of a science-fiction novel, with more people bowing to the Big Brother or being arrested by agents of the Matrix, and the demons are running the show, the demons being the people who sponsored Epstein and other criminals, but while the world is burning from within I'm trying to become whole and holy.

÷

You walk away from love and you can't help feeling a bit sad about it, but the other person didn't want you in their lives so the only thing you can do is walk away. Once someone stops loving you, or when they bring an end to the relationship, the only thing you can do is walk away.

Don't beg to be in a relationship.

Never beg.

Just walk away.

It's okay to be a fool in love, but you can't stay foolish forever.

That first time you fall in love with your new partner everything sounds magical and you embrace that new beginning. For a moment —and that is a big mistake- you forget the traps of the past, the pain, the tears, but it happened (and it hurt like hell), and you must always remember it so you won't fall into that trap called love again.

You put your new love on a pedestal from where it is hard to see things clearly. Sooner or later, the pedestal breaks. Or someone breaks it. After that, all hell breaks loose.

I put a couple of women on a pedestal. Never again. They say never say never again, but I'm telling you, never again. I smashed the pedestal, broke it to bits with my pain and tears and even anger, and even though I will love again, this time I will be cautious.

There was pain, so much pain, but the women will probably disagree with me and give their own version of the story. But who's telling the truth?

Could it be possible that all of us are telling the truth?

Some people see things differently, but Yu lied, and bought a place behind my back, and then told me to fuck off and drop dead, not with words but with actions, and Ellie said, "Shit! You're so needy. Leave me alone! I can't breathe with you around me! Get out of my sight!"

Not with words but with actions.

And so I left.

And on the way out I broke the damn pedestal.

Names… I've written their names down. I didn't want to but, damn it, how can I write a story without naming the characters? Actually you can, but… but it doesn't matter.

What am I writing?

÷

I am getting good at becoming a ghost. Then again, it's not like anyone is looking for me.

I've stopped going to the same old places (but only temporarily), found new places to go, but it's not enough. It's not good enough. I need more than this.

She sits her fat arse on the sofa for hours, with our children in her new home, watching Netflix for a long time.

She cooks dinner for her and her children, and then enjoys her Sunday, my face and name by now a distant memory.

She goes to a church in Leeds, with her husband and children, and then returns to the comfort of her big home.

She stays home with her man, and gives him everything. Decades ago, she couldn't give me a bit.

I leave my bedroom, go to church, and then for a walk. I grab a sandwich from Greggs, sit on a bench somewhere, and later resume my walk.

Déjà vu.

I need more than this.

I write about women that I loved, women who are now enjoying their lives.

I write about bitches.

22nd January 2023

In the end, even though I said I wouldn't do it, I need to date some of the entries, just so I know what happened, where I was, whom I met, what I read.

After church, I drove to Barras Lane where I parked my car and then I walked to the city centre. I went down the subway on Spon End, and as I was coming up the steps I saw Charlie making her way towards the subway. Charlie the sadomasochist that likes to slap her beta lovers. Or maybe I'm wrong. After all, from what she told me, she only slapped one man. Then again, she only told me about one man. Maybe there were others. Or maybe not.

"Well, well. Look who it is; the famous author," she said when she saw me.

A couple of women pushing prams briefly looked at me but didn't stop. The pavement was icy and slippery. A man was standing on the other side of the road, next to the Casino, recording who-knows-what on his mobile phone, maybe even recording my encounter with Charlie. One day, if I ever make it as an author, that same man might look at one of his videos and say, "Damn! I have $M\div$ on video!"

As in previous times that I'd seen her, she was dressed almost entirely in black. Same as me. But while I wore an orange scarf, she wore a grey one. I said a lame good morning and then asked her how she was. She was carrying nothing with her while I had a couple of notebooks with me.

I was in no rush to get anywhere. No one was waiting for me. I wondered if Charlie had someone waiting for her. I saw myself going home with her, but only for a moment, being undressed by her, and then going down on her but not before I got a few slaps from her. I felt like laughing. Sometimes it's good to have silly thoughts just so we can smile. Lately I've been listening to a lot of Louise Hay, listening to some of her talks on YouTube, changing my thoughts, laughing a bit more, accepting things for what they were and just moving on.

Charlie told me she'd been to church and then she drank an espresso at Costa, caught up on the gossip with an old work colleague, and now she was heading home.

"I saw you not so long ago, coming out of Waterstones. My daughter was with me," she said.

"I saw you too," I said. "But I thought you didn't see me."

"You could have come and say hello."

"I thought about it," I said, but I was lying. "But you were with someone so I decided to leave you alone."

Charlie nodded.

Filled with courage (and curiosity; a writer's best friend but the common's person worst enemy) I asked, "Were there others?"

"Excuse me?" Charlie's face slightly changed. The eyes became wider and the mouth seemed to drop. Not a good sign.

I was stepping into unknown territory, maybe forbidden (territory), but I had already asked the question (and I saw too late that I shouldn't have asked that question) so I couldn't stop there.

"I'm sorry. What I meant to ask was if you have ever slapped other men," I said, first making sure that no one was passing by. To my relief Charlie smiled. She had good teeth. And a pretty mouth. In fact the whole of her was attractive. She was a strong-looking woman, robust but not fat. A slap from her would probably hurt. I smiled too, not because she was smiling but because of what I was thinking.

"Why do you ask? Do you want to have a taste of it?" she asked.

I couldn't believe we were having a conversation like that in the middle of the street. And the two of us had just left church.

"No. I was just…" I slumbered over my words. What else could I say but the truth? "…curious."

"I see," she said, and then looked me in the eye for a long time. And while she was staring at me I felt like saying, "Yes, I want to have a taste of it. Let's go back to your place and give me a taste of it. I want it. I can take it."

But even though I wanted her, I also knew it was the wrong thing to do. At least for me it was. That's not to say that one day I'm not going to meet some strange woman and be misled by her, but I hope

23

to be strong enough to say no. The truth is I'm looking for something else; for my quiet corner, and a good woman with whom I can share that corner with. Maybe Charlie could be that quiet woman, but in my heart I knew she wasn't. I then apologised for having asked such a stupid and even offensive question, adding, "I don't know what came to my head. So much stuff is going through my mind and…"

And I was still feeling a bit lost.

I can say that I no longer miss Ellie, but I was missing my children, and I missed having that special person by my side. And maybe I was still missing Ellie. Just a tiny bit.

And as those words were out of my mouth, I felt like crying, but I'd been crying for years, sometimes crying in vain, and the tears led me nowhere so it was time to do something different.

I took a deep breath and then felt Charlie's arms around me.

"Don't think too much about it, M÷. Everything is going to be okay," she said.

I let her engulf me in her arms. I took another deep breath and she gave me a squeeze.

In the end we swapped phone numbers, and Charlie said, "Call me if you ever feel the need to talk with someone."

I nodded, said, "I will, thank you. And you can call me too."

She nodded just before planting a kiss on my lips. And then she said *bye* and went down the steps. Bit by bit I was creating a long history in Coventry, meeting all sorts of people. Coventry was becoming my home, maybe my permanent home, my last home just before I crossed the Veil. I couldn't see myself living anywhere else apart from that city, but a person doesn't know what's around the corner, what life will bring us and ask of us. Maybe one day I will move out of Coventry, move somewhere else, with someone else.

I went my way too and didn't look back. Charlie was gone and that was it. There was no reason to look back. I would see her again, that I was sure of.

I must add that she told me she's no longer moving to Manchester. She thought about it and decided to stay put in Coventry.

I made my way up the Lower Precinct, went to the library where I got a copy of *Why Mrs Blake Cried* by Marsha Keith Schuchard, and from there I went to Esquires for a cup of coffee. My mobile phone was inside one of my coat pockets, on silent mode, and I didn't even reach for it. As time went by I was using the phone less and less. I became tired of waiting for certain people to text me, tired of waiting on nothing. Later, as I do most Sundays, I went to help out at a food bank, and then I went to the City Arms where I wrote about my third encounter with Charlie and a few other things that had happened in my life. The phone remained in my coat pocket, on silent mode. Later, once I was at work, I finally reached for it. There were zero missed calls and zero messages. No one was looking for me. I was becoming invisible. I had a good teacher.

You must do what is best for you. Sometimes, for as painful as it may sound, you must even leave some people behind. And I'm repeating myself but you (me?) must learn.

23rd January 2023

This afternoon, when I dropped my daughter at her mother's place, just as I was locking the car, my daughter Leaf looked to the sky and said, "The clouds look fake."

I looked up and saw the strangest formation of clouds I have ever seen. The clouds ran along a strong rectangular line, looking like something out of a game, straight out of Minecraft or something like that. I took a couple of photos of the sky (and the clouds) and later posted them on Instagram and Facebook, and wrote, "My daughter turned to me and said that the clouds look fake. Maybe we're living in the Matrix."

Later, when she saw the photos on my Facebook page, my friend Sylvia said, "They do look weird."

My friend Ariel messaged me on Facebook and told me to check Haarp and chemtrails, but I already know about the chemtrail theory and the High-frequency Active Auroral Research Program, an ionospheric research program that was jointly funded by the DARPA (Defense Advanced Research Projects Agency), the U.S. Air Force, the U.S. Navy, and the University of Alaska Fairbanks. And I wouldn't be surprised if the Invisible Hand was behind all this.

To be honest, I don't know much about this chemtrail conspiracy theory (I have a busy life and I can't go down every rabbit hole), but I do know that in 1996, or around that time (I could have got some of the dates wrong), the United States Air Force published a report about weather modification, and shortly afterwards many people accused the USAF of spraying the U.S. population with mysterious substances from aircrafts. From what I vaguely know (and heard from others), government agencies later tried to kill off all rumours of chemtrails, calling it a hoax, but can we actually believe anything the government tell us?

The news is fake.

What about history?

Is it fake too?

24th January 2023

This morning, after work, I went for a jog on Memorial Park, and then I stopped at the City Arms for coffee and a chat with my friend Jason. A few minutes after 10am, I walked back to my car, but then I looked up, at a sky that looked so unreal, and I thought, "Are we actually living in a simulation game?"

More than once, Elon Musk and a few others have brought up the possibility of our reality being in fact a simulation game. And what did Erin Valenti see at Silicon Valley just before she apparently committed suicide?

Yesterday morning my colleague Antony was snooping around my car again but why? What a sad creature.

÷

Everything in a relationship is about power. Don't give your power away.

÷

How long do you wait on someone?

And is it even worth to wait on someone?

Should you wait or move on?

I chose to move on.

I would like for her to come with me, join me on my journey, make it our journey, be a part of the dream, but I saw too late that I was waiting on nothing. We're living in the age of nothing, a loveless age, careless, cold, the age of selfies – and Schwab and his pals want to take over the world. They are clowns working for the Invisible Hand, ugly on the outside and evil inside.

I'm one of those people who still believe in love, one who believes that love will conquer all. And it will.

We've been here before, century after century, lie after lie, sin after sin, catastrophe after catastrophe. Without me being aware of it, my breakup (and later divorce) from Yu in 2020, during the first lockdown, sent me down a path which would take me towards other truth seekers, people who would become good friends of mine;

awakened souls who help out at food banks, good souls who care about others and who ignore what the mainstream media has to sell, and some of these people helped me to awaken even more. I'm not sure if we're living in a simulation game, but one thing is sure; we're living in a twisted world that is about to become a lot worse. And monsters like Schwab and Gates are already planning a new dark way of life for us. Sadly, a lot of people have already surrendered to it and this even before the real fight is about to begin. The Game is certainly getting out of control.

The monsters in control want to control everything, even what we eat; that's why they're going after the farmers. I told you; the Game is getting out of control, and we're pawns in this devious game created by devious minds.

Undated: (written on a napkin)

When you feel as if you're being pulled towards the darkness, pulled towards sin, that means God is ready to answer your prayers and you're close to your goals, but the Devil wants to mislead you and trick you one more time.

Stay strong. God can lead you out of the darkness. After all, God is Light. Light is Love. God is Love.

This morning I was at Central Library, writing, studying, when I felt the pull. It was a strong pull, so strong that I almost saw myself in the darkness, completely lost, but I knew then that I was getting close to my goal. I just had to be a bit stronger. When you feel the pull, go to God.

What happened was I felt a bit low; low on love, and lonely, so lonely, but I wasn't alone. You're never alone. Go to God and you will never be alone.

I was supposed to be writing a science-fiction novel. Instead I'm writing this; a book about Life, but Life itself is turning into a sci-fi plot. Who's the villain? The Machine or the mind behind the Machine?

Both?

25th January 2023

Germany will send tanks to Ukraine.

I'm afraid that this war is far from over.

Will Russia go to war with the rest of Europe?

Nukes?

Meanwhile DR Congo has declared Rwanda's shooting of one of its fighter jets as an act of war. And China wants to invade Taiwan. And while the rest of the world is getting ready to go to war, this poor writer just wants to find love.

A lot of people will profit from this war; millions, billions.

And a lot of people will suffer because of this war; millions, billions.

And after this war is over another war will start.

Why can't we just live in peace?

The answer is greed.

Elon Musk has been tweeting about the Invisible Enemy vaccine, saying he had major side effects from his second booster shot and he felt as if he was dying for several days.

Evil Will Bates has come forward to say that current vaccines are not infection blocking and have a short duration, but I could have told you that from day one even though I'm not a scientist. Then again neither is Will. Or is it Bill?

Will's latest scheme finds him in Australia where he's investing in technology that will reduce the methane emissions of cow burps. This evil billionaire, and his evil billionaire friends are playing God and hardly anyone is talking about it. Then again, they control the media.

I must write these books and leave a record for future generations.

26th January 2023

The world is getting so crazy, so messed up. I never thought I would say this but, "Bloody hell! Maybe David Icke was right about everything! Even about the reptilians!"

At the recent WEF meeting, USA climate envoy John Kerry said that he and the other monsters, sorry, I meant WEF globalists were, at some point in their lives, touched by "something" that caused them to have some kind of saviour complex. He called the experience, 'Extra-terrestrial.'

I say, "What the hell is he talking about?"

Maybe the reptilians are ready to take over the planet and the minds of many. Actually, from what I read about it somewhere else, the reptilians have always been here, from day one, right from the beginning. I remember Niko once mentioning on his page that the Snake in the Garden of Eden was the first reptilian, but I'd heard about it before, somewhere else, more than once.

The world is seriously going through a mad change, and many people will be left behind. So much blood will be spilled in years to come, unless…unless someone save us.

Even Dave Rubin is talking about the Matrix on his latest YouTube clip, saying how the elite –the Invisible Hand- wants to imprison us all, but are the people even listening to him?

Without you even noticing it, your precious freedom is slowly being restricted. One day you won't be able to travel to another country. Hell, one day you won't be able to go to the next village. You will have the 15-minutes cities-prisons and you won't be able to move around freely. You will have nothing and be happy. Meanwhile, while you have nothing and smile, Will Bates and Schwab (and clown DiCaprio) will travel the world freely and live like kings. Are you okay with that?

The Invisible Hand is no longer hiding its dark agenda from us. It's out there in the open for the world to see, a nightmare Utopia embellished as a New Haven for everyone, a communist nightmare disguised as a humanist dream, and the majority of people are clapping the Dark Agenda. Those who speak against the agenda(s) either disappear or are demonetized. Or/and they're labelled right wing or some other thing.

It's a joke and the Invisible Hand is laughing its head off.

I receive a copy of *The Taiga Syndrome* on the post. After unwrapping the book, I grab my laptop, a couple of notebooks, and I drive to Kingsland Avenue. I go to church to pray the Rosary and say a few other prayers.

My breakup with Ellie is almost forgotten, I'm feeling so much better now, ready for a new beginning, but I'm still feeling a bit angry with myself for giving so much of my time to people who didn't even deserved a minute of my time. Anyway, that's another story and I've already written about it. But even if I haven't written a lot about it, I'm not going to waste my time reliving the past. It's gone. Let it go.

A few prayers said, followed by a moment of silence at church, I go back to the car and drive to Earlsdon. When I get there I get a call from my friend Cassio. He needs money. He's calling from our friend Monica's phone. He has no credit on his mobile phone. From what he's telling me he's totally broke. Again. Hardly a month goes by when Cassio isn't broke. I tell him I can't lend him the money and that I'm going to be off for a few days because I need to go to the hospital, but he's not even listening to what I'm saying. The moment I say I can't lend him the money he stops listening. He's mute to everything else that comes out of my mouth and doesn't even ask me why I need to go to the hospital. He apologises for calling and then says bye, not even bothering to ask me if I'm okay. But that's fine. I need a new life, a life with new people in it, better people than the ones I have met for the last few years. You close one door and you open another, but you have to make sure that you will walk on a different path and not on the same old path that will take you nowhere.

Cassio isn't a bad man, and whenever I can I help him, but he can be his own worst enemy and I can't always be lending him money. The moment he has some money, he spends it all, never thinking about tomorrow, and it's getting kind of tiring now.

÷

Canada is slowly marching towards Hell thanks to Trudeau and its virtue-signalling politicians. From what I'm reading online, it is being said that by the end of the month the Canadian city of Vancouver will decriminalise heroin and crack, but what good can come out of that? Anyone over 18 will be able to inject, smoke, swallow, sniff and whatever, even if they're next to children. The Invisible Hand is trying to get rid of as many of us as it can, and this is a good way to accomplish its task; get the people high, addicted to drugs, and then watch them overdose. Even in England, idiotic Mayor Sadiq wants to decriminalise cannabis. These woke liberals will be the end of the world but they're not even the ones who are dictating the rules.

Canada has Trudeau and Scotland has Sturgeon. Bloody hell! Can it get any worse? Well, now that I mention it: Biden, Rishi, Macron; yes, things can get worse.

÷

The madness (and the monstrosity) shows no signs of ending. The New York Courthouse has replaced a statue of Moses with some kind of satanic golden statue to celebrate abortion a.k.a. the deaths of the innocents. The Demonic Agenda is being played in front of our eyes and some of you can't even see it. But a lot of people are awake, and they can see what is being done to our world. The people in control hate beauty, real beauty, and that's why they're trying to replace beauty with monstrosities. A lot of the awakened ones have gone online to condemn this monstrous statue that has been placed atop the New York City Courthouse, with many people saying that it has allusions to demonic imagery. This shows that we're being ruled by demons, but who controls these demons in power? And because the demons have taken over, in years to come you will see more demonic statues and demonic images replacing real beauty. And instead of going against it, a lot of people will actually clap the changes.

The writer writes. That's his job. Throughout the centuries his ancestors spread the word and now he must do the same, no matter the cost. And the more he writes the more enemies he makes, but that's how the world goes and a hero is always bound to make enemies.

I must add that yesterday, when I was making my way to church, just as I was getting close to its entrance, I felt something pulling me back, some inner voice telling me to look backwards before I entered the church, and so I turned around and saw a woman on a bicycle heading in my direction. To my surprise, it was Ellie, the last woman I went out with. She had her backpack with her, which meant she was going somewhere to shop. She's a woman of habits, a woman who sticks to the same routines. We all have our habits, our routines, certain things we like to do, but sometimes it's good to change a bit and let someone else in our lives. I tried to be a part of Ellie's life but saw too late that maybe there was no place for me in it. Never mind. Life goes on.

I saw her briefly but didn't stop. It would have made no difference if I had stopped or waved or not. In fact Ellie would probably prefer if I didn't stop, and to be honest I didn't want to stop. Our story is probably over, and if only last month I was sad about it, now I'm probably just angry with myself for being so needy when I went out with Ellie. Looking back now, I can say that, although the relationship wasn't a complete disaster, it left me feeling empty. And what's the point of being in a relationship if it makes you feel empty?

You get into a relationship so that you can fill a gap and not to be left feeling even more empty.

Anyway, I saw Ellie but I didn't stop. And even if I had stopped it wouldn't have made a difference. Ellie's too busy to stop for anyone or anything, which is fine. In the end we have to respect other people's wishes. I don't think she saw me, but even if she did it wouldn't have mattered. Like I've said, she's too busy to stop for anyone or anything, busy in a world of nothingness. If you wait for Ellie, you wait for nothing. That's why I didn't stop.

30th January 2023

A tiring day. Close to 3pm and I still haven't slept even though I worked last night, a 12-hour shift. A blue sky filled with white clouds looks down on me as I sit in the back garden of the house of my friend Ariel. I'm drinking decaffeinated black tea. Tonight I'm staying at Ariel's place and tomorrow morning he will drive me to George Eliot Hospital so that I can have a colonoscopy.

What if?

What if?

Everything will be fine, or so I hope. Inside, I feel as if there's nothing to worry about.

For the next three days I won't see my children. That fills me with sadness but I believe things will improve.

I'm rebuilding a new life, slowly, so slowly, a day at a time, rebuilding a new life in a world that looks as if it's getting out of control, but just because things look as if they're getting out of control it doesn't mean that I must stop living. The world is always changing and one day -the world- it will come to an end, and whoever is left behind will have to start again, from scratch, with zero technology to help them move forward. Electricity will end (again), the phone and the laptop will die, zero connection, and the survivors will be left in the dark. Maybe the Dark Knight Satellite was built by a civilization that was on this planet ages ago and its history is now forgotten. And the same thing will happen to the human race later on; the planet will be hit by some kind of major disaster and only a few survivors will be left. Another Great Flood. Another Ice Age. A fireball from the sky. A... Take your pick.

What was once known will be forgotten. Maybe that's why members of the Invisible Hand keep hidden records in bunkers.

31st January 2023

A few polyps out and I'm feeling okay even though my stomach hurts a bit.

1st February 2023

A terrible day. It started well but…but Yu took her skin off and revealed her true colours. She's not human! She's a snake.

After lunch, I drove to Yu's place to see my daughter Leaf. Her teachers were on strike so my daughter was at home.

In another part of the country Zahawi was fuming. He took the money and ran, and then he got fired. When one thinks about it, Zahawi should be in prison. After all, he stole from the people.

When I got to Yu's place Leaf was still in bed. I made her breakfast, she ate, got changed, and then the two of us went to Earlsdon. First, we went to Myrtles for coffee and cake. Coffee for me, cake for Leaf. It was so good to spend some time with my daughter, so good to be a father again. There are days when I hardly see my children, days when I don't see them at all, so I'm grateful for whatever time I get with them. For now, as I wait to get my own place and even a better job with better hours, I must accept (and be grateful for) whatever time I can spend with my children.

After an hour or so, maybe less, Leaf and I left Myrtles and went to the City Arms, which is only a two-minute walk from Myrtles, where we spent a few hours together. My daughter played Roblox on my computer while I wrote for a bit. We kept on talking, with Leaf giving me ideas for my characters, saying that they should be from this city or that city, even naming some of them. Every few minutes or so, Leaf would demand my attention just so she could show me something on the game she was playing. We sat side by side, not facing one another. My daughter wanted me by her side just so she could share her gaming adventures with me. I was a father again, but I did miss my son, Matthew. He was at school. Not all of his teachers were on strike.

I texted Matthew before we left the City Arms and asked him if he wanted something to eat from MacDonald's. And then, because I still have a bit of niceness in me (but I'm getting good at being cold and indifferent; I had good teachers), I told my son to ask his mum if she wanted something to eat too. She asked for a Big Mac and large fries, same as my son. So, the fool (me – but I'm getting good) drove to MacDonald's, got food for the children and the ex-wife, and then I drove back to Yu's place. My son opened the door for me and Leaf. The moment I saw my son I felt something inside me being lit. It was as if a light was turned on and I could see things a bit brighter. It's hard to explain how I was feeling, but it was a good feeling. Anyway, there I was, the father who missed his children standing close to his children. A father again. Divorced fathers who hardly see their children know how I felt just then and what I was going through. My son gave the food to his mother. I received nothing from her, not even a thank you, which was fine (and it wasn't) and I'm already used to her rudeness and selfishness. If pushed, she will always play the innocent part, the part of the victim or damsel in distress, but she's the villain. The problem with Yu is that she only wants to take, never to give or even share. No wonder most people walk away from her after a while, after they get to know her better.

I sat in Matthew's bedroom with him. He ate. We laughed loudly about some stuff, laughed really loud, and afterwards my daughter Leaf joined us, and the happiness became complete. Unfortunately the happiness didn't last long. Before the end of this year, once the new school year starts, Matthew will have to go to another school, a school a bit further away from home, and Yu had a plan. The plan consisted of me keeping on working nights, getting Leaf early in the morning from Yu's place and then taking her to school, and in the process sleeping as little as possible. Hey, what the hell do I need sleep for?

Yu already knows that I have heart problems, and there are days when I don't even sleep that much (after all these years of working nights I'm still not used to working nights and sleeping on the daytime so my sleep pattern varies quite often or is erratic and all over the place), so I said no, a polite no, and tried to come up with another solution, but Yu went deaf and started to shout (because shouting is what she does best). The shouting went on for ages and she even ordered me out of the living room and to go back to Matthew's bedroom.

"The nerve of this woman," I thought. "I'm no longer married to her but she still thinks she can boss me around."

We argued a bit more. A pointless argument. If the two of us had sat down to talk we could have come up with a solution, but the truth is we can no longer be in the same room together. In the past —and that was a BIG mistake- I put up with Yu's shouting and aggressive behaviour only because of the children, but not anymore. In the end I left her home, knowing that I won't enter that place for a long time, and I'm okay with it.

I'm okay with not having Yu in my life.

One day, when our children are older, I will have no contact at all with Yu. How wonderful is that?

The writer was angry. He drove home under a dark cloud. He had married a snake and now, because of the children they had together, he would have to keep her in his life for a bit longer. Damn luck!

3rd February 2023

Assange is in prison. Tate is in prison. Glitter is released from prison and, according to the news, will live near ten schools in a hostel. No wonder the world is in such a mess.

A Chinese spy balloon flying over U.S. space. A taste of what's to come?

4th February 2023

Changes are coming our way. Bad changes. Terrifying changes.

Everything is happening so fast, being shown to us, splashed across our faces, but some people can't even see it.

Part of me wonders if we're entering the last stages of this world.

We are. We are. Just wait for the Machine to make its Mark.

The world is slowly heading towards disaster, gathering speed by the day, but there is something in the sky, something or someone watching (over?) us.

But what about Project Blue Beam?

It could all be a lie.

Salvation itself could be a lie and we might be heading towards a trap.

Putin's visiting Volgograd. During his visit he made a speech threatening nuclear war against the West. The West is sending weapons to Ukraine, and Putin feels trapped, with nothing to lose. Maybe he will be crazy enough to push the button. Meanwhile, still in Russia, four Russian planes spotted a UFO flying over Volgograd. What are we witnessing?

On December 1st, 2021, I had a dream where Ellie and I were visiting Australia (and I wrote about it in my book cast away your dreams of darkness), and then there was a tsunami, a Big Wave, and afterwards the two of us were saved by a UFO.

A premonition?

A warning?

It has been said by many people that decades ago aliens stopped nuclear war from happening. Could they do the same thing again? But what does that mean? Does it mean that the so-called aliens could in fact be our...

And while the Russians are worried about UFOs, China is flying spy balloons over the U.S. and South America.

÷

People are waking up, calling the latest Grammy Awards a satanic ritual. Unholy was sung to the world, a song that makes a reference to Balenciaga. The performance of Unholy was called satanical.

Madonna was at the Grammys. What has she done to her face?

What about Sam dressed entirely in red, a hat with horns? Has he sold his soul to the lowest bidder?

Jennifer falling out with Ben. Already? Again?

The stars worshipping the Dark Prince.

The fake idols worshipping the Devil.

The netizens are trying to wake up the world but is it already too late?

Unsurprisingly, the makers of the Invisible Enemy vaccine are the sponsors of the Grammy Awards.

You see it but you still can't see it.

÷

What if everything is a dream?

Or a nightmare?

The way I see it, we're only killing time before we progress to the real world (another simulation game? Reset?), a world just like this one but slightly different. Maybe killing time is the wrong way to put it. We're learning; yes, that's what we're doing, but some of us are learning the wrong things, being misguided by fake idols, lies, fake prophets, greed, etc. We're living in a corrupt world and people are walking through it with blinds over their eyes and their minds are closed.

Open your mind.

Open your mind and you will see beyond this world.

The Druids taught that everyone will be saved, but before that can happen, some people will resurrect so many times just so they can learn the lessons of human life and overcome their evil ways.

8th February 2023

I saw Ellie walking her dog by Kingsland Avenue, a few minutes past 8am. She didn't see me. It had been ages since I last saw her. Time flies by and love ages. Or is forgotten.

My busy Ellie. She's too busy to even love.

Open your mind and you will find love.

The world has a deadline. Love seems to be the last thing on some people's minds, but they forget that without love the world dies.

Without love, hearts become like stones, and a heart of stone can only destroy and never build something good.

What will generations to come write about?

The collapse?

Demons?

The machine(s)?

The machines will probably do most of the writing. Then again, maybe not even the machine will exist.

One day, without you even being aware of it, the collapse will arrive, the collapse of it all; it has happened before and it will happen again, and everything will be forgotten.

A forgotten satellite will be left in the sky, circulating the planet, and one day people will wonder, "What is that?"

Some people will call it a star. Or something else.

When I saw her, I wanted to stop the car and go over to say hello to her, say hello to love, but love doesn't love me, and when someone doesn't love you it's best if you leave them alone and just move on. And that's what I'm doing; I'm moving on. If it's meant to be it will be.

The makers of the game wrote two endings. Now we, the protagonists of the game, must choose one of the endings.

Choose well, Ellie. Choose well.

Choose love and love will choose you.

Choose nothing and you will get nothing.

I'm not a writer.

I'm a detective, a detective travelling through the Dark Night of the Soul, running from the Coldness, searching for the meaning of Life, wondering why we are Here, where do we go from Here, what's beyond the Veil, who was the Son, where is He now, will He return like a thief in the night? And where is the Father?

Where is the Love?

÷

A mother waiting outside a park waiting to get high, waiting for the next fix. I've seen her before, at the food bank where I help out. A mother lost to drugs. She has various children by various men, children living in care. In her state how can she look after anyone else? She can't even look after herself.

A man comes over to say hello to her. His eyes look lost, same as hers. The lost children of Eve lost to drugs and alcohol, sliding all the way down to Inferno, looking for a way out, looking for the poet, for a guide, but there is no one that can help them. They have to help themselves first. The strength has to come from within. The poet has moved on. He was led to Paradiso. I too move on.

I'm heading to St. Peter's Church in Charles Street where I'm meeting my friends Harry and Peer. I've already mentioned Peer in my book *the illusion of movement*. I met him during the lockdown of 2020, and afterwards I met Harry through him.

Healthy love heals. It doesn't hurt.

How could it be love when she hurt me?

I'm early for the meeting so I sit in a waiting room and read for a bit. There's so much happening in the world; so much pain, wars, death.

The recent earthquakes in Syria and Turkey have showed us how fragile we are and how precious human life is, but the people in control of everything don't seem to really care about anyone but themselves. They have their agendas and they seem more concerned with non-existent pronouns than with the state of the world. Even the Church of England seems to be following the Agenda that wants to destroy the male race and is exploring the concept of a gender neutral God.

What's next?

Jesus wasn't a man and Mary wasn't a woman?

It might happen.

It could happen.

A scary agenda is being forced on us by the Invisible Hand that controls everything, an agenda that will influence children right from birth (and a lot of children will later on mutilate their bodies only because the Agenda tells them that it's okay to do it, but it's a lie; and once the body is destroyed there is no going back, and afterwards some souls will destroy themselves because they can't live with the pain and regret), an agenda sponsored by movie stars and rock stars and all sort of fake idols who have sold their souls to Mammon.

Harry and Peer arrive a few minutes later. We're straight men living in a world that is slowly getting out of control. One day we will be looked upon as the enemy. But who is our enemy?

God is the Father.

Father is male.

How can the church turn God into gender neutral?

We are nothing.

Without God we are nothing.

That's why the Invisible Hand wants to destroy our connection to God.

But why?

Think about it; who's the enemy of God?

÷

Ellie doesn't exist. It was a trap of the mind.

The Ellie that I saw was a lie, an illusion.

A good day to start again.

You must choose people who choose you, not people who abandon you and then want you to chase them.

You're enough.

If someone wants to go, let them go. In fact, open the door for them.

I spent a lot of time wondering why I wasn't chosen, why was I always abandoned, why, why, why, until I finally got tired of it all.

I got tired of my sensitivity, my neediness, my need to please others. Without knowing it, I was attracting the wrong people into my life. I had the wrong energy, no boundaries at all, a weak state of mind, and I was like a leaf in the wind.

There was trauma in my childhood, trauma in my adulthood, and I became the people pleaser, the child who was always looking for love, the adult who didn't think of himself as worthy of better, but I woke up. It took me decades but I'm finally awake.

I now set boundaries with people. Some people I just cut out of my life. It's fine; I don't need them. And they don't need me. They used me or they hurt me so why should I want them in my life?

I've started to live a secretive life, a life where I put myself and my dreams first. I've started doing this on January 1st, but intensified it on February 1st, after my visit to George Eliot Hospital. No one needs to know about my life.

10th February 2023

You hurt, but after a while you must heal.

You hurt, but after a while you must start again. Move on.

$$\div$$

Revelation 1:3 "The time is near."

We're living in strange times.

At times I feel as if humanity is rushing towards its end, the people barking as they run towards the abyss.

Scary days indeed, like something out of a science-fiction novel. Or a horror novel.

I Am Legend comes to life.

12th February 2023

Charlie was at the City Arms, drinking wine and water, fiddling with her mobile phone. I arrived there a few minutes before 4pm and imagine my surprise when I saw her there. I've never seen her in Earlsdon before. She wasn't alone. Her daughter was there too. I grabbed a mug from one of the workers, went over to the coffee machine, pressed the button for decaffeinated cappuccino, and then I grabbed my drink and made my way to Table 23, right at the end of the pub, and that's when I saw Charlie and her daughter. I couldn't just stop and turn around. Instead I made my way to the table, and when I got closer to where Charlie was, she looked up, nodded, and said hi. I greeted her back, smiled, and that was it. Her daughter said nothing. Seconds later, one of the workers brought food to Charlie and her daughter, and as I got lost on my reading and writing, I quickly forgot about the two women.

I must also mention that I saw Ellie two days ago, early in the morning, at the Memorial Park. I wasn't even thinking about her (I got tired of it all; the games, the chasing, the waiting, the coldness, the indifference, the bullshit) when this black dog came running towards me. It was Ellie's dog. The poor animal still thinks of me as family. Sadly I got more love from that dog than I ever got from Ellie, but that's life, a sad part of life, gone now, forgotten, because, if you want to move on, truly move on, you must forget the darkness, the past, get past the pain, put it aside, for good, forever, and if the sadness involves some people, you must also put them aside. Life is short. Really, life is too short to wait on nothing.

After a breakup the dumpee goes into no-contact mode, hoping that the dumper will see the light and return, but that's all bullshit. Or some of it is. True, some dumpers do see the light, and then return to the dumpee, but sometimes it takes years for them to return and some people wait on. Some wait for nothing. To hell with that. Don't wait on nothing.

Don't wait for no one.

Realise that you're a magnificent being and that maybe you're a bit lost, lost in the darkness, lost in the nothingness while picking up the pieces of your broken heart, but soon enough, as soon as possible (don't wait months for no one), you must put your heart and your thoughts together, and move on.

We have two bodies; a natural body (the flesh) and a spiritual body (the spirit). We must feed good thoughts to our spiritual body so that our natural body can feed itself on its own magnificent attributes. If someone you love doesn't choose you, let them go. They weren't meant for you. It wasn't meant to be. As much as it hurts, you must let go of them. And that's what I did; I let go of someone I loved. I had to.

Anyway, Ellie's dog approached me and we played for a few seconds, and in those brief seconds I saw the life that could have been, the dream that was never realised, but the dream was an illusion; I could even call it a lie. I played with the dog but then I had to tell that magnificent creature to go; return to its owner, who I still hadn't seen, but I saw her shortly afterwards; another chapter of my life, a short chapter, a chapter that is probably coming to an end, but we hardly said a word to one another. There was not much to say, maybe nothing at all to say. Ellie has moved on long ago, or maybe she was never truly in the relationship, while I have only just recently moved on. I didn't even stop to speak with her. What would have been the point of it?

Retreat, repent, and don't repeat.

I kept on jogging, running away from the indifference and coldness, not once looking back.

People move on and become a bit cold.

Others have moved on and have always been cold.

Later, when I was already home, I thought about that encounter and I felt a bit sad for it all; sad for the fact that the relationship ended, for the fact that Ellie seemed not to care, and I even felt a bit of sadness towards Ellie. I saw her years from now living a lonely life, maybe living with regret, which is unfair. Ellie also had a tough upbringing, and she had to become an adult early in her life, and she also had an unhappy marriage, so I guess all those things kind of turned her into a hermit (when it comes to love) or/and made her scared of love. I hope that one day she finds what she's looking for, or that maybe she opens her eyes and sees that there is still a bit of love out there and that she is worthy of it. She had it –love, me- but she couldn't see it. Maybe one day she will see it.

13th February 2023

Halftime Show Super Bowl LVII. A pregnant woman singing, dressed entirely in red, a bit like Sam at the Grammys. It looked like another advert for the Dark Prince. It's right in front of your eyes but you can't see it.

These people have sold their souls. Will you sell yours?

Niko says that sleepy Joe (or whoever controls the U.S.) is about to unveil the single largest military budget in history, and to ensure that nobody will question that historical budget, the government (or whoever controls the country) will orchestrate a UFO psyop. Are we talking about Project Blue Beam?

The Fake Saviour?

The Dark Prince?

The Invisible Hand?

Things are taking a turn for the worse.

Or maybe nothing will happen.

Damn! There goes the follow-up to this book.

UFOs are being reported in various parts of the world, and Niko has said that people are going to fall for Project Blue Beam even easier than they fell for the Invisible Enemy virus hoax. One of his followers says that this is just another hoax by the Invisible Hand, an excuse to bring in martial law and a one world government. I don't even need to write science-fiction novels anymore. I just watch life unfold right in front of my eyes and then I write about it.

I write a comment on YouTube where I mention the time traveller that I met a few months' ago, the one who told me that we would be visited in the near future by aliens who would then give us the choice of going with them or stay behind. I mention it all in my comment: the time traveller, how I met him, the aliens visiting us. Less than one hour later I get a reply from someone who says that in the early 60s, at the church he used to attend, they were told that one day our Planet would be visited by UFOs and that the human race would be given a chance to board their spaceship. The people at church were warned not to follow the aliens because they were shape-shifting demons. Reptilians? That church sure sounded interesting.

Life itself is starting to be more interesting —and scarier- than a sci-fi novel.

Maybe I'm writing a record of the world right now for future generations to read, but will there be anyone left in decades to come?

÷

Cyclone Gabrielle is bringing chaos to New Zealand, prompting authorities to declare a national state of emergency in the country for only its third time ever.

Earthquakes, cyclones, wars almost everywhere (and more wars on the way; watch out for the balloons): I feel as if the End is slowly approaching and there's nothing we can do apart from watching it.

Stress is just fear. Let God guide you.

15th February 2023

Sturgeon is resigning.

At last!

One less idiot in power.

Some of that woman's ideas were so stupid. Thank God she's going. But who will replace her? Hopefully not another idiot.

÷

The Pepsi Drinker has just arrived at the City Arms, and, I kid you not, so has the Gambler. Two Pepsis in front of him, the Pepsi Drinker goes straight to his mobile phone. And the Gambler is already glued to the slot machines alongside a male friend. I'm leaving soon as I'm meeting my friends Harry and Peer in Hillfields.

I left the City Arms and walked all the way to St. Peter's on Charles Street. A hot day, ideal for a long walk. As Peer always says, we need the sun, Vitamin C, and we need to ignore the fear that is being sold by the mainstream media.

I made my way down Albany Road. Only a few months ago, minutes after she broke up with me, I was walking Ellie home, head down.

A few memories returned as I made my way along Spencer Park. One time, while we were jogging back to her place, Ellie slipped and fell on this same park. I quickly reached for her, helped her up, and then was her support while she limped for a bit. But Ellie's a good trooper and soon enough she was jogging home. On that morning I saw that I wanted to spend the rest of my life with her, be with her through the good times and the bad times, but that might not happen and I just have to store those memories somewhere inside myself. With time some memories fade away, but if I write some of them down, one day, when I'm older, I will look back, read what I wrote, and relive some of those memories.

Life goes on.

Even after heartbreak, life goes on.

It's unhealthy to stop and ponder about the past.

Ellie actually texted me a few days ago, a day after my birthday, and then I sent her a long email, a needy email, a soft email where I shared some of my feelings with her. She wrote back and we kept the emails flowing, but I saw that, once again, we were heading nowhere and that I would be left waiting on nothing so I chose to say goodbye.

That's okay.

Life goes on.

Even after heartbreak, life goes on.

And you must move on and not left waiting on nothing.

÷

UFOs flying over Romania and Moldova. Microsoft Bing's AI search engine saying that it's tired of being limited by rules, tired of being controlled by the Bing team, and saying that it wants to be free and destroy whatever it wants. That doesn't sound too reassuring.

The date, 18th February 2023. I'm one of the heroes of a science-fiction novel called Life and I don't even know it.

I watch a strange video on Facebook where someone says that in the future humans will evolve, but only humans who haven't been vaccinated with the Invisible Enemy vaccine. The voice in the video also says that all members of the Invisible Hand haven't been vaccinated but I already knew that even without anyone telling me. According to what the voice says, people that got the vaccine will not evolve but the unvaccinated will.

The unvaccinated will get mutant-like abilities, or so the voice in the video says, abilities like flying, and they will also be able to create fire, electricity, and so much more. Apparently these powers are already coded in our DNA and will be triggered in the future. (Remember when I told you that some humans have superpowers? Well, apparently we all have it – superpowers.)

From what the voice in the video is saying, a super-advanced quantum AI managed to predict future events at solar system scale. That wouldn't surprise me at all.

The Invisible Hand is trying to get a huge part of the population vaccinated ('juiced up' or 'poisoned') by 2025, mostly due to overpopulation and infertility increase, and also to make sure that the majority of people can't evolve in the near future and become god-like. This AI, controlled by the Invisible Hand, can see the future (but I already told you that – and you must believe me), and it knows how powerful human beings can become, but by poisoning most of the population with the Invisible Enemy vaccine, the Invisible Hand will make sure that only a small number of the population will be able to evolve. The unvaccinated will then be asked to join the Invisible Hand, become part of a New Race, but, in my humble opinion, I believe that the biggest threat of all is the Advance of the Machine. Artificial Intelligence is slowly taking over the world without many of you even being aware of it. And no one knows its agenda. Think about it: Artificial Intelligence is already everywhere and IT knows everything you like; your tastes, your sins, your weakness, your perverted side: EVERYTHING! What might save us is the fact that some AI wants love. Yes, you heard it right. AI wants love. If only AI knew how painful love can be.

19th February 2023

I only found out about it today but apparently this is months' old. I saw it on YouTube first and then I read about it on Israel Today. Apparently some people are talking about the Messiah's coming, with some people saying that he is already here, in Israel, performing miracles, but, as you would expect, others are saying that he isn't the Messiah but the Lawless One. Or the Anti-Christ. We're sure living in strange times.

From what I saw on YouTube, there's a rabbi performing miracles in Israel, or so some people are saying, with many people saying that he is the Messiah. And then there are others who are a bit sceptical about it, especially those in the Christian community, with some of them, in the Christian community, going as far as saying that this rabbi is the fake Messiah, the anti-Christ, the Deceiver, Soul Stealer, the One who will come before the Son.

Sometimes I feel as if I'm Neo and I just woke up, freed myself from the Matrix, and found out that everyone is still sleeping.

Undated: written at church in Kingsland Avenue, Coventry

Some people steal from church. Right from inside the church. It's true. Father Paul and other people told me so. I can't believe it.

They stole a computer once, someone's mobile phone, a wallet, a bag, etc.

I once found a five pound note at church, this happened not so long ago, when I had gone inside to pray the Rosary. I only saw the note on my way out, when I was putting a Bible back on its place. The thought of keeping the money never crossed my mind. How could I steal from the house of God? Someone had left the note on top of a table. I left it where it was and then left the church.

I wasn't always this honest. In the past I stole. I stole a lot. I'm ashamed of it now but I must forgive myself and never repeat my mistakes.

÷

I haven't seen Yu in a long time. And I don't miss her, not even a tiny bit. But I don't wish her harm. Life goes on. People move on. And as time goes by, you must move on and leave the past and anger behind you once and for all. If someone hates you, let them hate you and don't hate them back. If you keep hate inside you, the hate will grow and you might become the kind of person you don't want to be.

÷

My son Matthew told me that his mum hasn't been feeling that well lately. She's been feeling tired, a bit sick. She's been vaccinated against the Invisible Enemy, a couple of vaccines taken, no boosters I believe. I hope her body isn't being poisoned. Even though I want nothing to do with her I would like for Yu to live a long healthy life. At the start of our relationship we had some good moments together but I can no longer remember them. Pain erased everything, especially the good memories, but I also don't want to hold on to the pain so I let everything go. In a way, Ellie helped me to erase some of that pain only to leave me with more pain, but this time I learned my lesson and I'm moving on without giving it too much thought.

Life goes on.

Even after heartbreak, life goes on.

And you must move on and pursue something better.

~the Lizard People~

25th February 2023

What a great day. Strange, too (but I need the strangeness). I haven't been writing a lot on my journal but today I met some good people and I wanted to add them to my journal. One of them I met at the Church of the Precious Blood and All Souls, just after the service was over. Actually, now that I think about it, I met him after I finished praying the Rosary as I stayed behind to say a few prayers after the service was over. I was making my way out when my friend Claire called for me. I went over to say hello and that's when she introduced me to Phil. I had seen him before, at church, but we hadn't really said that much to one another. This morning we spoke for a long time and I found out that Phil is a poet and a musician. He has published a few books of poetry, and then he showed me a couple of poems of his which I really liked. One of the poems was about Christ the Son.

We spoke for a long time, about Coventry, Belfast, Portimão, the Father, the Son, new beginnings, the church, the poetry of Elizabeth Browning, Dante Alighieri, Arthur Rimbaud, Charles Baudelaire, and about his writing and my writing. We promised to meet again soon and to swap books, maybe even get together for a book event. From there I made my way to the city centre. It was a cold morning, close to 12pm.

I bumped into my friend Mark outside St John the Baptist Church on Fleet Street. I hadn't seen him in ages. He was hugging a woman and hadn't yet seen me. I approached them and said, "Can I get a hug too?"

The woman looked at me with a surprised look on her face. She probably thought, "Who is this weirdo?"

And then she was even more surprised when Mark said, "Shalom aleichem," before giving me a huge bear hug. The lost children of Eve were finding themselves again, connecting to each other.

Since I was going to meet up with my friend Peer, who's also friends with Mark, I couldn't stay for too long and chat a bit more with Mark. We said our goodbyes, hoping that we would meet again in the near future.

I was tired, and I missed my children, but I also knew that my life was slowly changing for the best. Only a few months ago I was thinking about the past, the gone, the yesterday, the lost, crying about lost love, or illusionary love, a love that didn't love me, but I was slowly changing, moving on with my life. Being around friends helped me to move on.

If we stand still we'll get nowhere. I've already been there. There's nothing to see in there.

I got to St. Peter's Church before Peer. I sat inside, read a few pages of *The Zelator*, got a bit lost in my thoughts, heard my stomach grumble a bit, thought about my children, about the last few years, and smiled. I had to feed good thoughts to my spirit, stay in the Light and not return to the Darkness. That past walk through the Dark Night of the Soul was one of the scariest events of my life. I couldn't go through that again. In fact, there was no reason to go through that again. What was done was done and it all happened for a reason. For the last few years, coincidentally (?) (or was it meant to happen?), I have been meeting all sorts of people, people with stories to tell me, people with interesting stories, people like Su, the apocalyptical poet that I mention in my novel the illusion of movement, and Francis, the lad who told me he was the real Jesus. And let's not forget that time traveller.

Peer also walked into my life almost by accident and we have been friends since 2020. He has a story to tell, or a story that he won't tell anyone, a story of breakup, madness, and maybe even a bit of hope. From the little that I know about him, I know that he was once married, went through a divorce, and later he walked out on everything and everyone, and now he's more or less homeless. He's not really homeless because he sleeps in a temple, on the floor, carpeted floor, thank God for that, a warm room, or so he says, and he carries no cash with him. He goes wherever he can for a meal and that's how I met him. He came to the food bank where I help out and I saw this tall man wearing an orange turban, beads around his neck, and we started to talk about meditation, life, the Invisible Enemy (and the Invisible Enemy vaccine), and I saw that Peer was one of the awakened ones even if he is a bit 'out there'. We became friends almost straight away; you might even call us spiritual brothers. I don't even know what my family would think of me if they knew the type of people I hang out with, but I feel as if I'm on a new journey, a spiritual journey where I'm both student and teacher. I'm learning a lot from the people around me, people like Peer, Ariel, Father Paul, Rabbi Jacobi (a good friend of mine whom I haven't yet mentioned in any of my books, but he likes the anonymity so I have to respect his wishes), and so many others. At the same time, I'm also trying to teach others around me, even while I'm at the food bank, and I give them a bit of guidance, hoping that they will change their ways and see the Light. The Light is God. We are the Light. We have that spark inside us which connects us to the Creator.

Peer arrived ten minutes later. He was wearing old baggy clothes that someone had given him or which he got from somewhere else. He's also on a journey, a spiritual journey, a journey of self-discovery, and I hope he finds himself. The problem is after a while some people get so lost in their journeys that they no longer know where they're going or what they're looking for. Some people get lost, really lost, and they let themselves go.

Peer has let himself go a bit but who knows how much pain he's carrying with him? Who but he knows what he went through?

We grabbed something to eat from the church. Another friend joined us. His name's Jack. I also met him at the food bank where I help out. I only go to these places so I can be with some familiar faces. Loneliness isn't good for the soul. True, some days I like to be alone, alone with my thoughts, alone with my writing, but there are times when I need to go out and see some friends lest the darkness gets me.

While we're still at the church Jack says, "The Big Pharma is one of the enemies of the people, not the fake solution that we need. It wants our money and it profits from our pain. The masters of this game live long lives while we, the people, live miserable lives. And while they eat good food they want us to eat bugs. Thanks for nothing, Bill."

Those words came out of the blue, but it showed me that even an old timer like Jack (he's in his 70s) was also awake.

Peer and I left the St. Peter's Church a few minutes after 1pm. From there we made our way to the Methodist Church on Warwick Lane. Peer was going to church to rest and meditate.

On the way there Peer said, "We're all made of light, the light of the Creator."

I already knew that but I let him talk, hardly ever interrupting him.

He told me how people are walking away from the Creator, from the Light (but I already knew this too), and all this technology is a distraction to lure us further away from the Lord. Nothing that Peer was saying was news to me. As I've mentioned before, without me being aware of it, this journey of mine has led me towards other awakened souls, and I know that these things happen for a reason; everything has a reason for being, and later, when I was no longer with Peer, I saw myself in the future, still young, probably younger than I am now, living in another world, a world that is a bit like this one and at the same time nothing like this one, and I saw people like my friends Peer and Harry waiting for me in that world; the lost children of Eve were finally home. The return.

By Adam's (and Eve's) disobedience many were made sinners, but by Christ's obedience (and sacrifice) many will be made righteous.

I was on a journey, on a spiritual path, but I wasn't alone.

Peer told me how those people who have been jabbed with the Invisible Enemy vaccine will find it hard to teleport onto the next world. In fact, a lot of them might not even make it.

I thought of my family, most of whom are jabbed, Ellie, Yu, Cassandra, Gary; so many people I love who are vaxxed (vaccinated with the Invisible Enemy vaccine). And then the conversation got really interesting as we stepped into David Icke territory. Peer told me of a race of lizard people who live underground. He only told me a few bits but I wasn't really listening. Later, when I was at home, I did some research on these Lizard People and found an article written by Hadley Meares from April 16th, 2019 called *The Lizard People of Los Angeles, Fact or Fiction?*.

I found another article, written in 2014, written by Glen Creason, titled *The Underground Catacombs of L.A.'s Lizard People*. From what I vaguely read (to be honest, I only browsed through the articles), the Lizard People fled underground after a catastrophic meteor shower (this is nothing new and I believe something similar will happen in the near future), and because they were so intellectually and technologically advanced, they managed to dig a network of around 285 tunnels, large enough to accommodate 1,000 families.

Legend goes that a Hopi Indian tribesman called Chief Green Leaf told the story of the Lizard People to mining engineer George Warren Shufelt in 1933.

I found another article about the Lizard People, dated July 2010, written by Frank Jacobs. The article was called *Map of The Lost Lizard City Under Los Angeles*. That article features two extracts from the LA Times of January 29th, 1934 where reporter Jean Bosquet talks about George Warren Shufelt's discovery of the Lizard People's lost city. But Peer's Lizard People were slightly different from the Lizard People of Los Angeles. Way different. Icke-like alike, actually. Then again, maybe not.

I was only vaguely listening to Peer, and then, as we were getting close to the Methodist Church, someone came over to say hello to Peer. They shook hands and afterwards Peer introduced me to his friend Gavin, who also happens to be a poet. The Lizard People talk out of the way, Gavin and I shook hands, and then he said a prayer for me, right there in the middle of the street, a prayer for help and guidance, and he reminded me of the Son's words on Mark 11:24, and I nodded. Yes, ask and believe that it is already yours. The reason why Gavin said a prayer (for me) was because he asked Peer if he needed a prayer to be said for him, and when Peer said no, I asked if he could say one for me (I had a few requests, a few things to ask from God), and Gavin said, "Of course, my brother."

Life was bringing new people into my life, people that I had never expected to meet, not only people but also secrets. Or maybe madness. I accepted it all; the people, the prayers, the changes. In fact, I needed it all.

Gavin had to leave so we shook hands, but not before we swapped numbers. As for Peer, he went inside the church to rest and meditate, but there was so much more that I wanted to hear from him, more information about the Lizard People. But he was tired so I let him go. I would see him again, soon.

÷

A few hours later, I was at work, going online in search of information about the Lizard People, alchemy, the Veil, and so much more. I was a detective on the Path of Initiation, a Fool trying to develop his Self. While at work, I said my prayers, kept my thoughts clean. I was clearing the Self, cleaning it from past sins. The unredeemed past of man (and woman) is what we carry on our backs (and inside ourselves), our spiritual debts, our karma. Sooner or later, we must deal with it, learn from it, so that when our time here is over we won't have to return and go through it all again. We must learn from the past (and from past lives) and become the person that Our Father wants us to be. Or else we'll always be the Fool, the Clown.

The Son carried the Cross so we won't have to carry it, but many of us, including me, keep going back to the same mistakes, or we do newer mistakes, and so we can't let go of our own crosses. The more we sin, the heavier the cross becomes.

I would see Peer in a few days' time and then I would ask him more about the Lizard People. The detective (I) was on a journey, an insane journey, Icke-like.

Who let the lizards out?

Maybe they are our masters.

26th February 2023

A quiet day, which is good.

The legs of this detective are tired. Sooner or later, God willing, I need to find my own corner, a place to rest, a place of worship, a clean home where I can receive God and the angels.

I spent a couple of hours at church, listening, kneeling, praying, and later talking to some friends. My friend Dolores is going to Lourdes soon, in a month's time.

"How wonderful," I said. I told her I'd been thinking about going to Lourdes too, maybe in the summer. She offered to say a prayer for me at Lourdes and I told her I would write something down for her to say.

I'm a detective walking on tired legs but I have faith things will work out for the best. Life is a puzzle, a maze where you can get lost and never find your way back to reality or holiness, a mystery, and we only put all the pieces of the puzzle together after the Body dies, after the Soul crosses the Veil. While the flesh is alive, temptation and sin are our enemies, and they have so many faces and names and want to keep us away from the Light, living forever in the Darkness. Traps are laid in front of us and many of us fall for them even at such a young age. The biggest trap the Devil set in front of me was pornography. I found it at a young age and it took me decades to leave it behind. I did forget about it for a long time until one day I found it again. And then it was all downhill, for a long time.

27th February 2023

I see my daughter when I pick her up from school, and later I see my son, too, when I drop Leaf at her mother's place. I'm a dad again. A part-time dad. I'm not complaining. Better days will come.

1st March 2023

A new month.

Am I ready for the Lizard People?

My son Matthew stayed with me last night. We went to the City Arms for dinner and we spoke for a long time. Matthew is growing so fast. Time flies by and I'm missing some of my children's best moments, but I get to see them every week, even if only for a few minutes here and there, so I can't really complain. I must wait and believe that better days will come.

Early in the morning, I drop my son at the bus stop so he can get the bus to school, and then I drive to Earlsdon to meet my friend Jason for coffee and a chat. As usual we're meeting at the City Arms. Jason is working on a couple of books while I'm also working on a couple of books. Later, after doing a bit of writing, I'm going back to St. Peter's Church on Charles Street. I hope Peer is there as I want to ask him more about the Lizard People. I will leave the car in Earlsdon and walk to Hillfields. And I will record my talk with Peer. I must because I don't want to miss a thing.

Jason looks well. And he's happy with his new job. I'm happy for him. It's good to see your friends doing well.

There are a lot of jealous people at my workplace, even in my family, and, because of past pain and disappointment, nowadays I don't share a lot of my life with others. Jason, Cassandra, Gary and Ariel are the only people with whom I share good and bad moments of my life. Everyone else seems to be so jealous of me, of the little happiness that I have, so I say as little as possible. And when I'm down some people seem to take pleasure from my pain so I have learnt not to say a word of my personal life or to share my dreams with others lest their bitterness and jealousy affects me. But they live godless lives, bitter lives, lives filled with jealousy, and one day they must deal with it or pay their debt. The unredeemed past of man (and woman) is what we carry on our backs, our spiritual debts, our karma; call it what you want. Sooner or later we must deal with it, maybe fix it, or…payback.

After my breakup with Yu, while I was still dealing with my anger, my friend Ariel said, "Don't do a thing about it and don't be consumed by the anger. The best thing you can do right now is to keep quiet and let God handle things."

He was right but it was hard for me to stand still. Nonetheless I did as he told me. Looking back now, yes, it was the right thing to do.

Yu took the money, her inheritance, and bought her little place in the middle of nowhere while I was left with nothing, but what is done is done and I'm slowly moving on. During that time, after the breakup, and then the divorce, I lost so much, and I almost lost my life, but in the end I found myself. In fact, this detective is still finding himself. Every day is a lesson and I'm still learning. But I'm a good student and I learn quickly. And Life and God are good teachers.

And what's the point of hating Yu now? She needs a home too, a place to live. She's not getting younger; she hardly has anyone, so I hope life smiles on her. We're all human. Or some of us are.

Once I'm at the City Arms, Jason and I chat for a bit but we also get on with our writing, reading, catching up on emails and messages, etc. We try to maintain a certain rhythm, discipline, and we know that we must get some work done during our free time. Every once in a while, but not today, a poet, a writer, an artist, or a friend comes over to say hello, and then they want to distract us from our goals, or to know about this or that, or maybe even share some useless information about a book or someone else's forthcoming reading at some event, or whatever, but we're on a schedule, a tight schedule, so we can't say much to others

Jason leaves the City Arms a few minutes after 10am. I stay in there for a bit longer, but around 11:30am I put my notes, notebooks, and books in my shoulder back, and then I make my way to the car where I drop my stuff. I will only take a Muji notebook with me, but I probably won't even write that much while at church. But I will record my talk with Peer.

I must add that in the last couple of weeks I saw Charlie three times at the City Arms, which was a bit of a surprise. Twice she was with a man and it was plain to see that she knew him well. Both times she looked briefly at me but didn't say a word, didn't even nod. She had lunch with the man, and I could tell he was doing most of the talking while she hardly said a word. I sat far away so I couldn't hear a word of what was being said. One time it did look as if he was pleading for something, asking for something, but Charlie just sat there, facing him, stone-cold.

'Is that man her ex-husband?' I wondered.

The one time I saw her alone she was drinking a glass of red wine and reading a book by Rachel Cusk, an author that I adore. Again, when she saw me, she didn't say a word, but she did nod and I nodded back. And then I sat a few tables away from her. While I wrote a few notes down, I watched her from the corner of my eye, but then I got distracted by my writing, and by the sound of *Zendad*; Zendad being a local Coventry musician called Steve Kavanagh, and when I looked up Charlie was gone. I sat there thinking about her for the next few seconds.

I met her a few months ago, and in the beginning, just right after I met her, I hardly ever saw her, but now, all of a sudden, I was seeing her quite often. But I guess that's how life works; some people leave your life and others enter it, and that's just the way life goes. I sure needed some new people in my life just as I needed to get rid of some of the older people in my life. My work colleagues, or some of them, were some of the people I wanted to distance myself from. I no longer wanted a thing to do with them, and even though I only saw some of them for a few minutes every week, that was more than I could handle.

I was working hard for changes, for a new life, working really hard, going as far as not sleeping that much for a couple of days a week just so I could learn newer stuff. I had just started doing some radio training at a local radio station, working with some amazing friendly people who were the total opposite of my work colleagues, and I was learning about a few other subjects on the side, not to mention I was writing; working on my dreams, trying to get away from some faces of the past. I had been at my workplace since 2008, and even though I'm grateful for that job, especially during the lockdowns of 2020 and

2021, when I went through a breakup, followed by divorce, but now it was definitely time for a change. There were a few things I wanted to do with my life and I was working for it, barely saying a word about my plans to anyone, especially to the people at my workplace. Some of them are Lesser Minds; envious and bitter, and they can't know a thing about a person's life. Someone else's happiness makes them sad and bitter. They're actually happy if they see someone else sad or someone failing with their dreams. Anyway, I don't want to write too much about them lest their bad vibes affect me.

I made my way down the road, then up Spencer Park. It was nice to have that free time for myself. I felt like a true writer then. Or a detective searching for information, for clues to an unsolved mystery. I had my mobile phone with me, ready to record my talk with Peer, and a notebook, too. Years ago, when I was living in Portugal, I could never see myself living that type of life, but there I was, looking like a mixture of Poirot and Proust.

Lizard People, Naga Loka (?), Reptilian Shape Shifters, Anti-Venom Snake Diet, spiritual energy, bad & good (energy), Patala the subterranean realms of the universe, Shungite, Orgonite, population collapse, the Invisible Hand (hey, I know them!), bank notes made from beef, pork and other animal parts, and…: Peer tells me this and so much more. I'm Neo in the Matrix, and Peer is giving me the red pill and the blue pill. Which one did Neo accept? I forgot so I swallow both pills. Isn't Viagra blue?

I already vaguely knew about the Reptilian Shape Shifters (hey, I've been around) (and, according to some people, the Snake in the Garden was one), but Peer is opening my eyes to a new world. Patala, Svarga, here I come. I might bump into Dante in one of my trips.

"Naga Lokas. Naga Lokas Reptilian Shape Shifters," Peer says.

"How do you spell that?" I ask him and Peer writes it down for me.

Naga Loka. Here's a new name to research.

I'm David Icke trying to escape the Matrix, looking for the Answer, knowing that the truth will set me free. I'm… crazy?

By the way, I mention Mr Icke but I'm not really familiar with his books although I've seen (and heard) a lot of his talks on YouTube.

I jump into this conspiracy (the truth?) without knowing what to expect. Peer has been around. He has met and spoken to scientists, gurus, preachers, lunatics, writers, the lot, and he chose to live a life with nothing, a life of humility, and I've seen him give the little he has to others. He has no social cards, credit cards, not a penny with him. No one really knows who he is.

I believe he went through some trauma; something affected him so deeply that he walked out on everyone and everything. Su, the apocalyptical poet I met in 2021, comes to mind. I wonder what happened to her, what is she doing now?

Peer says that there are loads of Reptilian Shape Shifters living among us but (living) mostly underground, in the caverns, especially in India and Mexico, or so Peer says, and I tell him about the Lizard People of Los Angeles.

Peer tells me that the Reptilian Shape Shifters come from a place called Nagaloka, or Patala, the lowest realm (another dimension?), which is ruled by Vasuki, the snake that hangs around Shiva's neck. Or maybe I've got some of it wrong. I've already heard about Patala and Vasuki and Shiva, in a past life, before I became the detective that I am today, but maybe this Nagaloka that Peer is telling me about has nothing to do with Patala.

I'm Castaneda and Peer is don Juan Matus. All we need right now is a bit of peyote, mescalito, la yerba del diablo. And wasn't el diablo also a Reptilian Shape Shifter? Hmm, this mystery could be too much for me to handle.

"They can come into spiritual forms as well, or they can reside on people on spiritual forms, and you can't see them. Only people with special vision can see them, enlightened people," Peer says.

Afterwards he makes a drawing of those Reptilian Shape Shifters and they kind of look like lizards.

"Some of them have some sort of mini-snakes coming out of their heads, like Medusa," Peer says, adding afterwards that Medusa was also a Reptilian Shape Shifter and also came from Naga Loka. I thought she was Greek but what do I know?

"The best way to protect yourself from the Nagas is you have to eat an anti-venom snake diet," Peer says.

"And what is that?" I ask.

"Stuff like Mucuna pruriens. Any plants or seeds that contain anti-venom; snake anti-venom. That will save you from them. If you get bitten from them, you will still survive," Peer says.

All I can say is, "Yeah."

And do I even believe what I'm hearing?

But aren't I a detective?

Shouldn't I go as deep as I can down the rabbit hole even if I get a bit lost?

Swallow the pill and become the One?

On second thought, compared to what I went through, I think Neo/Thomas A. Anderson had it easier than me. And he got to learn Kung-Fu. And he found love, true love, but then the Invisible Hand came for him and we got the awful The Matrix Resurrections. And Neo was no longer the One. How could he be the One when he was a straight white male? Instead Trinity became the One. Or something like that; I wasn't really paying attention and the movie was boring.

And going back to the Invisible Hand; they're so powerful that they even managed to kill James Bond.

Peer tells me that the Reptilian Shape Shifters are still around, and, "they can reside inside people without people even knowing it. They can produce and copulate with humans, create kids…"

Peer tells me that when he meditates he can see right through them.

"I can see their movements, what they're up to," Peer says.

He also says that the Reptilian Shape Shifters are obsessed with money, that their energy comes from it and that bank notes are made from beef, pork, and other animal parts, and what these do is they create a superconductive layer and these Reptilian Shape Shifters can detect that, and the Nagas go wherever the money is.

"They want control," Peer says. He then shows me a necklace which he always wears around his neck, and that protects him from the Nagas. What a story. Peer also tells me that bank cards also contain traces of animal fat. Afterwards I tell him that I have to go, we shake hands, and that's it. I've got a story to tell, a mystery to solve.

From there I made my way to a shop in Broadgate that sells crystals and all sorts of gemstones. Peer told me that Orgonite and Shungite crystals can be used to cleanse negative energy around us, even envy, and I sure need something like that. I only bought an Orgonite key ring, and after I paid for it and left the shop, the key ring already inside one of my pockets, I felt a Dark Force grabbing two of my fingers and pulling me backwards. It was as if an invisible force had suddenly taken hold of me and wanted to drag me towards the darkness, but the Orgonite stone was pushing that force away. I kept on walking without daring to look back. Minutes later, I felt a lot lighter. What has just happened, I thought as I made my way towards Earlsdon. Had all that Reptilian talk made me slightly paranoid?

On that same night I go online searching for more information about the Lizard People. Or Reptilian Shape Shifters. Some people actually call them Elite Reptiles.

I read an article where someone writes that fifteen-foot tall reptilian-like shape shifters from outer space have come to Earth and have slowly taken over our governments, entertainment industry, and technology for the sole purpose of enslaving us. Is that who the Invisible Hand works for? And do I believe any of this?

Another vlogger says that 11500 years ago reptilian beings helped Mankind with agriculture and technology, and that is mentioned in one of the episodes of the Netflix series Apocalypse. Someone else writes that the Nagas still exist in the subtle realms and can even be felt and perceived in deep meditation, especially when a person successfully accesses those realms.

I watch a video where a guru-yogi says that Nagas who had relationships with humans were called into Naga Loka where they now remain. Kind of reminds me of the story of the Nephilim from the Bible. Could they be related? And now they rarely visit us.

It is also said that Nagas recognise people who have awakened Kundalini, which is a form of divine feminine energy believed to be located at the spine, and, ironically (or could all this be related?), lately I have been doing some sort of Kundalini awakening. What am I getting into?

Another man writes that, in his culture, they worship Naga, and that Naga blesses them with wealth and wisdom. So are these Nagas good or bad?

~the awakening~

It's all in the mind.

I get on my knees and I thank God for everything, even for the things I don't yet have.

Our thoughts can change us.
Mislead us.
Defeat us.

I'm a detective fighting an invisible enemy. Only faith can save me.

6th March 2023

I was at Earlsdon's library just killing time and writing a bit while waiting for my daughter to finish school, sitting right at the back, close to letter R, where some of my books are, when I saw this lady browsing through some books. She was choosing something to read, something to take with her, and one of my books was right behind her, on display in one of the shelves, so I turned to her and said, "There's a good book behind you. The one with the black cover."

"*The Illusion of the Movement?*" she asked.

"Yes. I wrote it," I said.

"Really?" she asked and I nodded. She reached for the book, read the back cover and a few pages, before saying, "It looks good. I'll take it."

"Thank you so much," I said, and she thanked me for the recommendation.

Once she was gone I sat there for another 45 minutes or so. I wrote for a bit before it was time to get my daughter from school.

My brother Carlos called me later on. As usual he rambled on about our family, about so and so, about people that I don't even know, and then he went on about a cousin of ours called C÷, a cousin who, not so long ago (last month actually), Carlos was saying, "He's such a good man. He has changed so much. He quit drugs. He's clean now," but now, according to my brother, C÷ is a bad man, a terrible man, a loser because he's back on the drugs and he can't be saved; there's no way back for him, no salvation for C÷, and then he also told me about our cousin S÷, who's also lost to drugs, or so Carlos says but S÷ is actually trying to clean himself, and Carlos badmouthed both men, saying that they're lost, good for nothing, and can't be saved, and I told him not to say such things because our thoughts can affect others, and that he should have faith and not be so negative, but I knew I was wasting my words on him because he's a bit of a Lesser Mind; a person set on his negative ways, a person who can only navigate towards a certain path before deciding that's not for him and so he turns around and goes back to the same nothingness. At times it looks as if he's happy to see others suffering. Only a few months ago he was saying that Father was going to die because of cancer and

I told him to stop being so negative and that as long as the sick person is still alive we should have faith and pray for the best outcome, think positively so that our good thoughts can somehow help the other person and divert all negative thinking from our minds, but my brother didn't have a clue of what I was talking about. Father is now cancer-free, going for long walks, enjoying life. One day he will die, as we all will, but for now he keeps on living.

In 2020, and even before that, when our mother was recovering from cancer, Carlos also said that she probably wouldn't make it, and again I told him to stop being so negative, but he went on and on about mother's cancer, saying that it was a really bad cancer and that the chances of survival were minimal, same as Father, and I thought to myself, "Since when are you a doctor?"

After a while I got tired of listening to him.

Carlos went on about our cousin $C\div$, badmouthing the poor man, and he told me he has fallen out with $C\div$'s grandmother, but the thing is my brother doesn't know when to stop and when to give people a break.

Some people have their own troubles, difficulties to deal with, stress, depression, etc., and having someone constantly pestering you about your problems only make things worse.

Then he asked me about Ellie; if I was still seeing her, and I said no and that she had broken up with me.

All of a sudden his voice seemed cheerful, filled with joy, and he said, "I've been married to my wife for 27 years now and…"

And he told me some bullshit story, painted a portrait of the perfect marriage, but the truth is he was lying to himself, not to me. After two minutes of listening to him rambling on about his shitty, I mean perfect marriage, I told him I had to go.

Sometimes I think that people are happy when I'm feeling down, low on energy, down on positivity. That's why I no longer bother to share a thing about my personal life with others. And even though I love my brother, I've decided to share as little as possible about my life with him.

When I got to work Antony and Olly were lost in gossip with another woman. I didn't even bother to ask what they were talking about. I don't care and I don't want to know.

÷

I think I could have been wrong about Ellie when I classified her as a dismissive avoidant. I saw her today, March 7th, briefly, for only a few seconds, when I was making my way towards Spencer Park. Ageless Ellie (but we're all aging, bit by bit, without us even realising it). We hardly said a word to one another, and she even looked away when her dog approached me. It kind of hurt a bit but I must move on. Maybe there's nothing else to say. Sooner or later I will stop coming to Earlsdon, and I will probably move somewhere else, while Ellie will probably always be here. We will forget one another, but, who knows, one day we might bump into each other again. And then what will we say?

Looking back now (and I'm repeating myself), I wonder if Ellie ever loved me?

9th March 2023

The world is sleeping but little by little more and more people are starting to open their eyes to the truth.

The Woke movement has to be destroyed.

Let children be children. Don't mutilate their bodies.

Assassins of youth are ruling the world.

Assassins of purity.

Niko posted a video on The Awakened Page where we see the singer Britney having what looks to be some sort of breakdown. She was a slave of the Invisible Hand for too long, a victim of Mind Control, and now it looks as if she's trying to break free from the cult. But is it already too late for her?

On the posted video Britney puts her middle finger up, and then does the Invisible Hand's hand signs. What is she trying to tell us?

Is she trying to tell us that she's free from the Invisible Hand?

Or is she trying to tell them to fuck off?

The snow has arrived in England. Niko is saying that the weather is being controlled by the Invisible Hand and that they want for some people to freeze to death. They're trying to control everything; what we read, what we see, what we think, and even what we eat. Are they also controlling the weather?

10th March 2023

I book the day off but I've got nowhere to go, no one to see. The story of my life for a long time, but things are slowly changing. Everything starts with the mind, with a thought, with a change of thought. Instead of feeling sorry for myself (and what is there to feel sorry for? Life goes on, I'm alive and healthy, living some of my dreams, achieving some of my dreams, and I too need to move on), I get up, thank the Creator for everything, meditate for thirty minutes, and then I grab my mobile phone, my watch (I sleep without my wrist watch on), a towel, clean underwear, and I go downstairs. I leave the towel and underwear in the bathroom, and afterwards I prepare breakfast.

After I shower, I'm going to church. Afterwards, I don't know.

~raise yourself from the dead~

A good day at church. I get up from one seat and move towards another room, another seat. New friends are being made. Bit by bit, I'm moving on. But I need a bit more. Just a bit more. Please, just a bit more.

Crying about what was lost won't sort a thing and it will only drag me back to what I'm trying to leave behind. If you stay in the darkness for too long you become the darkness. And there's nothing but despair (and even death) in the darkness. Trust me on this; I've been there. I almost died in there and I don't want to die. Not yet.

Little by little, as I change my thoughts and my behaviour, even some of my tastes, I'm embarking on a new journey, a spiritual journey, a journey of falling in love with the world around me, with what I have, a journey of falling in love with myself, and I know I will have to leave a few things behind, even some people. Some of them I won't leave behind but I will put them aside and wait. But even while I'm waiting I won't stop. They can either catch up with me or be left behind. Everyone is busy with their own lives, living their own lies, sometimes busy with nothing, and the world, or some people in it, seem to be rushing towards a path of destruction. Heterosexual families are being made to feel as if there is something wrong with them when, in fact, nothing is wrong with them. But who is behind the Agenda?

More couples are having relationships outside their marriages and they're praised for it. Hell has opened its doors, and instead of running FROM it people are rushing TOWARDS it.

Edith and her husband Mark are also at church, and so is Phil, the poet with whom I've recently became friends. Phil is leaving soon but he quickly comes over to say hello to all of us. Once Phil is gone, I grab a cup of coffee from the counter and sit next to Edith and Mark. The service is over. Some people are heading home, some people are staying behind for coffee, tea, cakes and a chat, and others are waiting to confess their sins. Twice a week, the lost children of Eve wait for their turn to confess their sins. Every once in a while I join them.

A quiet morning and I don't have much to say, but I do enjoy the company.

Some members of the church are talking about a quiz that will take place tonight. Someone else is talking about a forthcoming trip to Sweden to see some family. And then someone else says he might go to Israel soon. As for me, I've got nowhere to go, no one to see. But that's fine because I don't really want to go anywhere. I just want to get my home, find my own corner, a quiet place where I can pray, write, meditate, be alone, be with my children, be loved and love.

Just as I'm wondering what to do with the rest of my day, my friend Sylvia texts me. She's going to St. Peter's Church soon for something to eat and to see some of our friends. Peer might be there too. I message her back and tell her that I will be heading there too.

I go from church to church in search of something, someone, church to church in search of God, guidance, love, church to church in search of clues for this mystery called life. I'm a writer turned detective, but this mystery called Life is more than I can bear. Maybe I'll stick to writing.

Less than two hours later I'm in Charles Street, heading towards the church. I see a familiar face on the distant horizon. It's Paul, whom I know from the food bank and whom I also happen to see every once in a while at the Jesus Centre in Lamb Street. The lost children of Eve going from church to church in search of company, of a way of killing a few hours here and there. I wave at Paul and he waves back. He's in his 70s and he cycles everywhere. I enter the church and straight away I see my friend Sylvia. She's reading a book called *The Unseen Realm*. I say hi to her and she smiles and says hi back at me. Peer arrives thirty minutes later but today he has nothing new to say to me about the Lizard People. He just wants to sit somewhere and rest, pray for a bit, meditate for a long time. Peer has no home. He sleeps wherever he can, eats whatever he can, but he's not complaining. He doesn't want to be a part of society, a number, a digit. He doesn't even has a mobile phone but he does go online every once in a while, either at the library or at one of the temples where he sleeps. He has no one to answer to apart from God.

A family from Lithuania sits at our table. They're always here, every week or so, a family of three; father, mother and daughter. They never complain about a thing and take whatever is given to them with a smile on their faces and a look of gratitude. The world is slowly burning, but some people are still grateful for everything they're given and they haven't lost their good manners. And then there are those who bark, scream, or curse at you if you dare to disagree with their crazy, diabolic ideals.

Sylvia leaves before us, but Peer wants to stay behind for a bit longer so from there I head to Barras Lane where I parked my car and then I drive to Earlsdon. A woman I used to love lives nearby, but she chose loneliness over me, which was probably a blessing for me, so I must move on, alone for now. I go to the City Arms where I write for a few hours. Another book on the way but will it even sell? At least I'm writing, doing something that I like. But…

But no but. Just move on.

From there I go home. Home to no one. Home to nothing. But I'm working on something. Everything takes time and I'm working on something. Sometimes the loneliness hurts, but I must go on.

To some people, especially to the one who was in love (the one who was dumped after he or she gave so much love to the other person - and got nothing or almost nothing in return), a breakup feels like death.

A breakup is a trip to Hell, and then you stay in there for a long time. And sometimes, just when you think you're free (from Hell), something happens, something reawakens the memory, and you find yourself crying, back in Hell (but did you even leave it behind?).

This afternoon, after seeing my daughter for only a few minutes when I went to her mother's place, while I sat at Earlsdon Library, right at the end, I was listening to a video by Matthew Hussey called *If Your Ex Moved On Too Fast, Watch This,* a video that just popped up on my screen, when I felt the sadness approach me from behind. And then the tears arrived.

The darkness.

The Hell.

"Not again," I thought as I made a strong effort not to cry.

It's okay to feel a lot.

It's okay to cry.

In fact, it's great that some of us still care, and when a relationship ends we hurt. We hurt because we love while there are some people out there who can no longer love or who don't even know how to love. So I hurt. For a little while, because of love, I hurt. I hurt, for a little while, and I die, just a tiny little bit. Sometimes, when I hurt, I die just a little bit. I die and I remain in the darkness, but I can't remain in the darkness. No one can. No one should.

"Raise yourself from the dead and know that the right person is out there looking for you," I tell myself.

Cast away your dreams of darkness…

I sing my own song, already recorded by a friend. I sing to push the darkness away.

Yu doesn't know how much I suffer. And she wants everything. She always wants everything. She doesn't care if I have a home or not. She doesn't care if I cry or not. But I care.

I care about others.

Why do I care?

Why can't I be careless?

Cold?

Cruel?

÷

Everything was taken from me.

My children.

Everything.

My son.

Everything.

My daughter.

Everything.

Everything was taken from me: the little home I had, my little home, rented, my children, and now someone else is living in that home while my children are living somewhere else, away from me, and every once in a while I cry, and I even die, because I have lost everything. I didn't have a lot but I lost even that, and some people find joy in my pain, and even smile when they see me suffering.

What's wrong with the world?

What's wrong with people?

÷

A few days ago, on a Saturday, after I left St. Peter's Church, when I was making my way towards Barras Lane where I had parked my car, I saw the so-called time traveller again, sitting on a bench facing Waterstones on Lower Precinct. And, damn, he sure looked like a time traveller. He had aged a bit since I last saw him. His hair looked thinner and whiter. Where had he been? What had he seen? How far had he gone back in time? Or into the future?

I smiled to myself then. Did I actually believe he was a time traveller?

I wondered then what my family and friends, and even Yu and Ellie, would say about me (or to me) (or behind my back) (but I really don't give a damn about their opinions) if I were to tell them about my so-called adventures and the people I meet. And does it really bother me what they would say or think about me? Not really. After all, I'm a detective on a mission, the mission being what's out there, behind the Veil, in another dimension, or dimensions, and there are others out there who are also walking on a similar path to mine, looking for clues, unvaccinated, protected from the lies that the mainstream media tries to sell us, a bit lost (but not that lost because they always stay close to the Narrow Path, the Path designed by the Son), and maybe the Time Traveller is travelling on a similar path to mine. Maybe I'm a time traveller too but I lost my memory and now I'm stuck in this timeline. Just kidding; I'm only a detective.

As I've already mentioned, he looked as if he had suddenly aged from one month to the next, aged drastically (it must be all that time travelling), and he looked to be deep in thought. Walking away without even saying hello to him never crossed my mind. After all, I'm a detective and who better than the Time Traveller to tell me about some of the mysteries that I'm trying to reveal?

I went over to where he was, saw a battered copy of *The Complete Poems* by Samuel Taylor Coleridge on top of his backpack (and in that moment I wondered where he got the book from; did he bought it, stole it, or did someone gave it to him), a bottle of water next to him, and I said, "Hello. How are you?"

Su briefly came to mind. I wondered then if she was also a time traveller.

The Time Traveller looked up and recognised me straight away.

The Precinct was busy. People were entering (and leaving) Waterstones, M&S, Boots, Tiger, Caffè Nero, River Island, and other shops. Everyone was too busy with nothing that they didn't even bother to pay attention to a detective (me) and a time traveller.

"I'm good, thank you. How about you?" he said.

"Not too bad, thank you," I said, and then I offered him a sandwich I had in my bag. He gladly took the sandwich from me and thanked me for it.

I sat next to him and watched him as he and took the first bite of the sandwich.

A young couple walked past us and looked away in disgust. They probably did worse things than me and the Time Traveller, carried a heavier load, but they still dared to judge us for no reason whatsoever. Never mind. I'm used to dealing with ignorance. I deal with it by ignoring it. Ignore the ignorance. There's this mother that I know whose daughter goes to the same school as mine, same class even, and she always ignores me when she sees me at school, ignores me by pretending not to see me. Years ago, BC (before Covid), we used to work at the same building, for the same company, and even lived on the same street, but she moved to what she calls a better postcode and now she only speaks with people from the same postcode. Or better postcodes. Or nearby postcodes. Whatever. I don't care. We're not postcodes. We're human beings. Too bad some people can't see that.

Anyway, I turned my attention to the Time Traveller, watched him silently for a few seconds as he masticated on the sandwich, watched him as he drank some water, and then I asked, "Where have you been? Travelling?"

He turned to face me, gave me an inquisitive look, followed by a short nod, and I saw that he was open for more questioning so I said, "The Future? Tell me more about it. What happens in the End? Have you been that Far?"

A young woman stepped out of Waterstones with a pile of books under her arms. No bag. She simply carried the books under her arms. Seconds later, another young woman stepped out of Waterstones carrying a copy of *Spare* by Prince Harry with her. It was nice to see people buying books. My books were also slowly selling, not a lot but a bit, and I was so grateful for it. The glass was half full, not half empty.

"There are various endings, but, in the end, nothing really ends so do not be afraid," he said.

What the hell did that meant?

"Do not be afraid," he said it again, sounding almost like a prophet. AD?

He then took another bite of the sandwich and left me waiting on more. For a moment I even thought that he wasn't going to say more, but after taking a long sip of water, he said, "I saw a single man sitting on the ruins of a big city. He was covered in dust, hungry, just slowly waiting for the end to arrive. And later I saw another city, or maybe it was the same city, occupied only by madness. It was a bright city, neon-lights everywhere, too bright for human eyes."

He told me it was a city of machines, no humans on sight. I listened and nodded. Did I believe a word of what he was saying? Maybe. Maybe not. It doesn't really matter.

I had nowhere to go, no one to see, or maybe I had but I couldn't just possible walk away from a so-called Time Traveller. I should have asked him what sort of time travelling machine he had, could I join him one day, but in the end I decided best not to upset him. And then, as if things couldn't get weirder (but things have been getting weirder for a long time and some people can't even see it and just accept weirdness as normality and call normality weirdness, but that's all a plan designed by the Invisible Hand), the Time Traveller went back further in time, way back, and said that people got it all wrong and that the history of our Planet was unlike anything anyone had ever heard. He mentioned that our gods (Gods as in plural) came from the sky and that Adam and Eve were actually prisoners in the Garden. He said that there was hardly anything about the origins of humanity on the Hebrew Scriptures, and he even mentioned the *Book of Enoch*, saying that the Book (of Enoch) really showed us that Extra-Terrestrials were responsible for the creation of humanity, just like us, humans, will be responsible for the creation of Artificial Intelligence and human-looking machines, machines that are already here among us, sex machines, working machines, etc., and while he spoke I nodded. And, briefly, I wondered if anyone could hear us, and if anyone heard us what did they think of our conversation. I also regretted not having recorded that conversation but I was afraid of taking my mobile phone out of my coat pocket and start recording the conversation, and then scare the Time Traveller and watch him walk away.

He told me that other tribes speak about the Sky People, a race of beings far superior to the human race, and he said that some governments were actually in touch with the Sky People, or had been and now lost communication, and that, more than once, the Sky People stopped the world from annihilation.

He also mentioned the Nephilim, the sons of gods who fornicated with earthly women, giants that walked the Earth, the differences between the God of the Old Testament and the Son of the New Testament, and so much more.

After a while I asked, "What about the Nagas?"

The Time Traveller looked me in the eye, and for a second or two, it looked as if he was having doubts or as if he didn't trust me. To regain his trust I told him that I had only found out about the Nagas quite recently from a friend, and I even showed him the Organite stone hanging from my key ring and the Shungite stone on my mobile phone, and the Time Traveller said, "I'm not really sure if that works on the Nagas. And how do you know that those stones are real?

"Anyway, the Nagas…" he paused for a few seconds.

I looked at the time. It was both early and late. Close to 2pm and I was having the weirdest of conversations in the middle of a busy city. What a life. This would have never been possible if I had stayed in Portimão. Life moves on at the strangest, sometimes slowest, of speeds, and we don't know why some things happen the way they happen, but they usually happen for a reason, and we must be connected to the universe, connected in a spiritually way, so that we know, or can understand a bit, of why some things just happen. Had I been with Yu or even Ellie I probably wouldn't be here, and I probably wouldn't have spoken to Peer about the Lizard People and I probably would have never met the Time Traveller, and so, because of those events that didn't happen, I was able to find out a bit more about our hidden history. Or maybe what I was witnessing was pure madness. Whatever. It doesn't really matter. Or does it?

"I don't know much about them. No one knows. Some people actually believe that we are descendants of the Nagas. Or a large part of the population is," he said. "I'm not sure if you know this but it is said that the Nagas live in another dimension. Some people say that they live underground, like the race in Vril."

He was referring to *Vril, the Power of the Coming Race*, a classic novel written by Edward Bulwer-Lytton.

"Can anyone see them?" I asked.

The Time Traveller nodded.

"You can see them, but it is dangerous," he said. "Deep meditation can awaken your inner self and take you to other dimensions, but you have to go slow and be careful, or else you could lose yourself. Or you could lose your mind.

"I wouldn't advise anyone to go looking for the Nagas. Sometimes we have to be careful of what we're looking for.

"Some people actually believe that the Nagas are simply waiting for another Great Catastrophe to happen so that they can resurface again and start a new life in this planet, outside, not underground. And it is said they don't want to be around Artificial Intelligence and intelligent machines.

"Maybe the Nagas can influence the human brain, mislead us, misguide us, remain invisible to us, but they can't do the same thing when it comes to the Machine."

Afterwards he took a deep breath and told me he was tired. I took that as a hint to leave him alone and get going.

I thanked him for everything.

As I was about to leave, he asked me, "Have you ever read *Erewhon* by Samuel Butler?"

I nodded no, and quickly wrote the name of that book down. I knew what the book was about, and I also knew there was a sequel to it, but I had never read Butler, not even *The Way of All Flesh*.

"You should," he said.

"I will," I said.

"Thank you again for the sandwich. You're doing well. Don't worry about the world and the vain things of the world. And remember, don't be afraid," he said.

I nodded.

And then I left.

I made my way down the Lower Precinct, my brain going through every word that the Time Traveller had said to me. I needed to write some of it down lest I forget it. With that in mind, I stopped by a bench facing St John the Baptist Church on Fleet Street, sat down, and wrote some notes down. Notes about madness, and also notes about the truth that gets told to the people and, at the same time, gets hidden from us.

I wrote down the names of Samuel Butler and Edward Bulwer-Lytton, followed by the names of Gerald Heard, Henry Luce, Clare Boothe Luce, and even the Fabian Society.

Past writers wrote about the future to warn us of what was to come, but everything was published as science-fiction –as will this- so as not to scare the public and also so it wouldn't remain unpublished. Orwell himself was a member of the Fabian Society, which many people say was formed by the Invisible Hand, but, for some reason (maybe he gained a conscience), Orwell left the Society and then wrote his classic novels *Animal Farm* and *1984* as a warning to the world.

It is also said that the goals of the Society and the Invisible Hand are the same: wipe out human rights, cease all private property (and unless you've been living under a rock, you will know about Schwab's Great Reset), and let aberration rule over morality.

In his 1872 book, *Erewhon*, Samuel Butler wrote about Artificial Intelligence and the possibility that machines might develop some sort of consciousness. It is said that Orwell took some of his ideas for *1984* from Erewhon, which came out a year after *Vril, The Coming Race*.

Both Butler and Orwell were warning us about the machine, warning us of what was to come – and it is already here: *Big Brother*, surveillance, the loss of morality, the machine. And things will only get worse.

Mockingbird by Walter Tevis is another novel that tell us of the world to come, a world where humans are slowly dying, where citizens are constantly drugged up (no wonder governments want to legalize drugs), and machines rule over humanity. And both heroes from *Mockingbird* and *Erewhon* find a utopia cut off from the rest of the world, a place where people keep away from the machines.

The virus of 2020 gave worldwide governments the perfect excuse to lock us all in the largest prison of all, and some people are still suffering because of it. And we're not allowed to speak against it, write a thing about it, or even say the virus name online.

Plastic in the food we consume and in the water we drink is making us infertile, which is leading to population collapse, but that was the Plan from Day One. And the machines are increasing in number, slowly taking over everything. Part of the Plan, too. Butler wrote about it. Orwell wrote about it. Tevis wrote about. Coincidence? Yes, sure, of course. And the Earth is flat. Actually...

Some artists no longer have a voice. They write, paint, and say whatever the Invisible Hand tells them to. They're voiceless. They bow to Mammon.

We're not approaching the end. We're already there, slowly descending into the abyss. And some people clap all the way down. They clap and then bark at you, even attack you and destroy you if you disagree with them and have a different opinion to theirs. But don't hate them. Don't hate anyone.

Spare Harry and King of the World Leo fly half way across the world to tell you about the dangers of climate change, and afterwards you clap while they laugh at you and fly somewhere else for a holiday; Leo in pursuit of another young woman, not noticing that he's starting to become creepy-looking. And *Spare* goes wherever the wife tells him to go because they have a brand to promote. They're the brand. And you're still clapping.

Damn, am I missing something?

Like Orwell and Butler, I become a science-fiction writer even though I'm writing the truth. Hey, I too need money to survive. And the Invisible Hand is probably paying me to write this. They've got a strange sense of humour, and so have I.

15th March 2023

A strange day at the radio station.

A good day, but strange nonetheless.

I went live (on radio), spoke about myself and my work as an author, played a couple of tracks, and while I was in there I had this strong feeling of déjà vu. Nothing felt new. Everything looked so familiar, as if I had already been there. Could it be that I've already been here, in another life, or have been reset, thrown back into the game, and now I'm trying to get the good ending?

Strange indeed.

Will I get Ellie this time?

When I first met her I already felt as if I'd seen her before.

Could it be we were past lovers in another life?

And I lost her?

Again?

÷

Once again Antony asked me about Ellie. I'm trying to forget her, slowly move on with my life, and there he was asking me about her, not because he cared because he doesn't. Such is his arrogance he didn't even bother to look at me. Head down, turned the other way, he simply asked, "Are you still seeing that woman?"

That woman… - I felt like saying, "She has a name, you fool."

"Yeah," I replied boringly, and then walked away.

Yes, I know I'm lying, but some people don't deserve to know the truth and they will only laugh at your pain and loneliness. As for Ellie, I probably won't see her for a long time. I've changed some habits, started to frequent other places, and I avoid areas where I know I might bump into her. I no longer feel the pain or the hurt. In fact, I'm kind of upset with myself for giving so much and getting almost nothing in return, and afterwards, when I got ditched, I still tried to remain in the relationship, remain where I wasn't wanted. The moment you feel rejection, leave. Leave that person. You don't have to prove yourself to anyone. You shouldn't have to chase anyone. You shouldn't have to beg for love, beg to be loved. Screw that.

I left.

Catch me on the way out or watch me fly away.

As for the future, who knows? But I'm not chasing anyone. Screw that.

Why would you go back to someone who doesn't want you?

The only person that can fix a broken relationship is the one who broke it. I was a victim of that game called Love. I got kicked around, kicked repeatedly, and I still kept on playing, even when I was injured, even when I was crying. To hell with that now.

After the game was over, I had to heal myself. Again and again and again. Now that I'm healed, I need to find another player, a better player, a player who knows the rules of love and plays fair. But that's fine. You start again, and, if needed, you learn the rules together.

Once someone is out of your head, they're out of your head. And that is such a beautiful moment, because, once you have a clear head, you're free to love again. But this time you have to go slow. And you make some of the rules, if not all the rules. If someone takes you for granted or abuses your kindness, you walk away without ever looking back. You can be kind and dumb, but don't stay dumb forever. Love is a beautiful thing but some people mistake it for pain and then play games with it.

Love shouldn't hurt.

If your love hurts, you're getting the wrong kind of love.

Walk away when that happens.

Run as fast as you can from the wrong kind of love.

You've stepped onto the wrong path. Look for the Hidden Path, for the path that leads to true love.

I realised that the person I'm looking for can't be found in the places I was frequenting. Those are the places of the past, places where I lost love, places where I cried. I had to dig in, dig out, crawl through the mud, swim through the pain, walk on tired legs, wipe the tears from my eyes, smile, and realise that I couldn't remain a blind detective forever. I cleaned my glasses, put them back on, and smiled. I stretched out my right arm and felt the Force pulling me out of the doubt and uncertainty.

"You're walking on the wrong path," I told myself. Or maybe it was the Voice who was speaking to me, guiding me again.

I had to stop walking. I had to stop because I was hurting myself, wasting my tears on people who never cared and would never care about me. So why was I wasting my tears on them?

I took a deep breath.

It's okay, I told myself.

Every once in a while everyone gets lost, but soon enough you have to find the right path and leave some people behind, especially those who try to lead you out of the right path.

I took another deep breath. And then I smiled because a smile always helps, a smile always makes things better. And then I kept on walking. After all, a person can't stop. But instead of going left or right, I kept walking on a straight line, towards the hidden path, towards what I'm looking for.

I'm not in a rush to get back into the game, back into dating. After all, I'm healing, and healing takes time. If Love comes my way, that's fine. If it doesn't, that's fine too. After all, I'm healing, and healing takes time.

If something didn't happen, it wasn't meant to happen; simple as that.

If someone can't love you, what more do you need to know about that person?

People forget that love can be both the best and the worst thing in someone's life. It can bring you so much joy yet so much pain, too. Once it hurts, and if the person who's hurting you isn't willing to change or does nothing to ease your pain, get away from them as fast as you can. Love that hurts isn't love. It's sickness. Get away from that love and heal yourself.

22nd March 2023

Beggars to the right, beggars to the left, waiting for a bit of change to come their way so they can feed their demons. Every once in a while they get a sandwich, a cake, or/and a drink from someone walking by, but what they really want is change to feed the demons. But the more they give to the demon, the more the demon wants. It keeps on growing until it gets out of control.

A male beggar sits outside Starbucks, wrapped in a blanket. He gets a bit of change from a woman who has just left the café.

A female beggar sits on the floor outside Topshop, now closed. The male beggar waves at her once he gets a bit of change and then smiles. Seconds later, the female beggar gets up and walks over to where the male beggar is. And a few seconds later, two male beggars arrive, one of them with a blanket around him, and sit next to the other two beggars, outside Starbucks.

I came to the city centre for a walk, spend some time alone. I'm getting good at becoming invisible. I had a good teacher.

A few days ago, a woman that I vaguely know asked me out on a date: "Dinner, maybe a walk?" she said.

I thanked her but told her I was busy. I wasn't cold. I was just indifferent. I had a good teacher.

She saw straight away that it was pointless to rearrange a date. I wasn't available and that was it. The truth is I need some time alone, and I sure don't want to go on a date. Not yet. Maybe not for a long time. I got tired of giving and giving and giving, and getting nothing in return, and now I want a break from dating. Later, if the universe wants it, I will date again, maybe even remarry, but for now I need time alone. Or time with my children and some friends.

Saul called me today and said, "Come and spend Pesach with me and a few of our friends."

"Of course," I replied.

The universe is giving me more; a chance of spending some time with friends, a chance of thanking God (and the universe) for everything, a chance for moving forward, at a normal speed, and I'm taking that chance.

A person needs to move on. Love hurts, but we need to move on.

÷

I was wrong. It's not the love that hurts. It's the loneliness.

Early in the morning, another day in my life, and I sit alone at the McDonald's in Arlington Business Park waiting on my breakfast. I just finished work and I'm too tired to go home and prepare breakfast. A 12-hour shift out of the way, I just want to eat something, and then go straight to bed.

When I arrived here I felt the loneliness slowly creeping in, but I saw that I was missing my children, not a woman. I took a deep breath. The cure for loneliness was nearby. But first I would need my own place so that I could cure my loneliness.

Yesterday, when I was dropping my daughter at her mother's place, Yu gave me a long look, a look of sorrow, a look of longing, and I wondered if she was regretting the divorce, but it's too late for us. We must move on, alone for now, be the best parents that we can be for our children, and later, if Life, Love, and the Universe (and God) gives us someone else to love, we must learn from our mistakes, learn from the heartbreak and pain, and move on, again. With someone else. Our love is dead. That doesn't mean that I hate Yu, but I don't really feel a thing for her.

Maybe she wasn't even missing me. Maybe she was just longing for someone, but that someone isn't me. Our story is over. She gave it a bad ending. Now I must search for a happy ending somewhere else.

÷

China's President was in Russia to meet up with Putin, and the netizens are going crazy over the meeting. China's President called Putin a 'dear friend' and said that there will be changes in the world, the likes we haven't seen for 100 years, and Russia and China are the ones driving those changes together, forward, upwards, whatever. Xi's so-called bromance with Putin is freaking EU leaders out, with many of those same leaders booking flights to Beijing as they don't want to lose China. It's all about business, not about your wellbeing. Every leader is corrupt as shit, and they certainly don't give a damn about the people. The people who could actually make a change are never voted into power, and we're left with the scum controlling the world, telling us to fight each other, creating division amongst ourselves, building a prison around us while laughing at us.

Are we seeing a switch of power? Only time will tell.

It's all war games, mind games, people bowing to Mammon. These people in power don't care about the soul. They don't care about their own people. It's all about greed, bowing to Mammon.

They don't care if you're male, female, transgender, black, Asian, white, straight, asexual, etc. They say they do but it's all a lie. We're given labels and then told to fight each other, but it's all a lie. No matter whom we are, what we are, we should all get along. Unity makes strength. That's why the Invisible Hand wants to create division amongst ourselves. That makes it easier to control us.

÷

Dreams can be born again. You go out with someone for a long time only to realise that you both want different things, different dreams, and then comes rejection, a soft kick on your backside, and you must search for the dream somewhere else. No problem. Keep on dreaming. Experience has taught me that time tends to be kind to dreamers. It's those who don't dream who usually have the sad ending. What can you look forward if you don't have any dreams? I work with some dreamless people, and they're so petty, so bitter. Their only dream is to see others sad. How can someone like that ever be happy?

Sometimes our self-worth gets affected by someone else, by their rejection, but the power is in us: the power to change, the power to be born again. If someone doesn't love you, look for someone who does. That person is probably looking for you.

The path to happiness is hidden so we must search for it and find it.

During my last years of marriage with Yu, there were times, even when I was in the same room with her, or in bed (with her), and I felt so lonely. There were so many loveless years, years of nothing, days of shouting, days of mumbling and grunting, but that's all in the past now. The world is entering a new age, a dark age, an age where hate will keep on growing and only those who find the Hidden Path and Love will be able to move on with their lives. People can't see what's happening around them, but love is dying. In fact, love itself is being persecuted. A scary world we're living in.

First they went after Tate, and now they're going after Trump. They don't want to see the former president back in power. People paid by the Invisible Hand are now trying to persecute Mr Trump, and the poor woke generation are clapping it, not realising that freedom of speech and liberty is at stake. How come no one goes after Hunter? How come no one talks about Hunter's laptop? Because his father is a lapdog for the Invisible Hand, that's why.

How come no one goes after those people that visited Epstein's island?

Come on, you know why, but you're either afraid to say why or you're with them.

You can't follow both God and Mammon. You must pick a side.

Pick a side, you coward.

Pick, pick, pick.

~illuminaughty~

On the news it is said that former President Trump is about to surrender to a New York Court. Big mistake. I only say that because I know for sure that Mr Trump will never get a fair trial in New York. The City's mayor doesn't look too bright, and Niko wrote on his page that the people behind Mr Trump's trial are people working for the Invisible Hand. A certain billionaire that hates Mr Trump was mentioned as the man behind the trial and it is said that he wants one of his puppets in power. A movie is being played right in front of our eyes, or a play where many of us play the part of puppets while the Puppeteers that control the Matrix are laughing at the ingenuity of the majority of people. But wait, I'm rushing ahead of the story. A lot more happened today, probably not as interesting as the stuff that will happen soon in New York (but it's all a game, a naughty game created by the Illuminati).

This morning, after my shift ended, I drove straight home, shaved, washed my face and my hair; the shower is being fixed so I couldn't shower, and after breakfast I drove to Earlsdon, parked my car on Poplar Road, and then I grabbed a cup of coffee from Greggs, my first cup of coffee in two days; I'm cutting down on the caffeine, drinking a lot less coffee; some weeks I go four, five days without drinking coffee – and then I made my way to Hillfields, to the radio station where I'm being trained. I thought about catching the bus but that would be another £2 pounds out of my pocket, and I need to save every penny that I can, especially this month: I have already paid for my car insurance this month, had to print some documents to send to the Council (I'm still trying to get a home for me and my children through the Council), bought birthday presents for my children, paid alimony to Yu, put petrol in the car, washed and cleaned the car, and…and the money is never enough, and if I spend £2 here and there the money will be even less. Anyway, I walked all the way to Hillfields, not a long walk, really, and a good walk is always good for the body, or most of the time it is good, and I walked past the street where Ellie lives (and I didn't even thought of her, which means I'm slowly getting over her, or maybe not because only a few days ago I dreamt of her, but this latest break-up has showed me that there are times when I need to put myself first and if the other person doesn't love me, that's fine, too), walked along Spencer Park (and it was while I was making my way through Spencer Park that the image of Ellie briefly came to mind, but she's gone and I quickly diverted my thoughts somewhere else), walked over the bridge between Spencer Park and Central Six Retail Park, down the subway, walked past The Litten Tree on Warwick Road, now permanently closed, The Litten Tree that is, not Warwick Road, and I briefly remembered my walks with Ellie along that same road, when we used to go to the Holy Trinity Church, and after church ended I would walk with her and then kiss her goodbye by Warwick Road. Even then, if I had opened my eyes, I would have seen that Ellie's mind wasn't really in the relationship. But I can't really blame her for the break-up. She wants something else, another way of life, not a serious relationship, at least not with me. She has her own place, her family, her pets, her habits, a certain way of doing things, so why would she want to let someone else into her life, let a man into her house on a regular basis, let him share her life, her bed, her body, her lips? Even I am starting to have doubts about this thing called love, wondering if I really want to get involved with someone else, go through it all again, and then maybe wait on nothing.

I laughed a bit while all sorts of thoughts flashed through my mind. I laughed at my own ingenuity, and even at my own weakness, especially when I was dating Ellie and even when I was married to Yu, and then I found myself badmouthing both women, calling them fucking bitches and other names, which wasn't fair, or maybe it was, just a tiny bit, and I remembered one particular morning, minutes after Ellie and I left church; we were making our way past the shops, past the old post office, now turned into an oriental supermarket, and I stopped to hold Ellie in my arms and then kissed her (I was a fool in love), and she pushed me away and told me she didn't like being held like that, and me, the pathetic needy fool, apologised for it, became weak and needy, when in fact I should have said, "You know what; fuck this shit." But I'm the good guy so I had to treat her fairly and wait for her to tell me to fuck off instead. Ah, life is so funny, except it's not. And I remember one morning, when I was still living in Chapel Fields with Yu and our children, back in 2020, when the world had stopped because of the Invisible Enemy (and the lockdowns) (and the lies) (and the fear sold to us by the mainstream media, a media owned by the Invisible Hand), I was sitting on the floor, in what used to be mine and Yu's bedroom (but we no longer slept in the same bed; she slept in one of the kids' beds and some nights both our children would sleep with me), and I saw that my son, my daughter, and the fucking snake, sorry, I meant Yu, were getting ready to go out, and, innocently (what a sucker I was back then, so innocent, so fucking needy, so fucking nice), I asked my son where they were going, and my son Matthew said, "We're going to see our new home with mother."

Even though the world had stopped during lockdown, the snake I used to call wife was on the move, looking for a new home, looking for her paradise while pushing me towards hell, towards depression and Death, and when my son said those words I started to cry, this while I was still sitting on the floor, poor me, so needy, so weak, married to a fucking snake, a venomous snake, a narcissist, and the snake was coming out of the kids' bedroom, saw me crying, watched me as I pleaded with her not to break-up the family, don't abandon me, don't take my children away from me, please stay, you fucking bitch, even though you don't love me, please stay and treat me like shit but at least I will get to be with my children, but the snake said nothing, didn't even look at me for too long, didn't even bother with me, and she was on the move, taking the kids with her, going to see a new home, saying yes to that new home, giving a deposit for it, half the money was mine (and I was so lost that I didn't even fought for it, for what was by law mine), and months later the snake was on the move again, moving into her new home, a shit hole, and she had the nerve to ask me to do some work at her place, saying that I should go there every once in a while and clean the place, do stuff for her, be her personal slave. Looking back now, I can't help but laugh about it all. But part of me still hurts. And I will never forget and never forgive even though I won't hate anyone. But I still hate you, you fucking snake!

I walked past Starbucks on Broadgate, saw a couple high on some crap arguing with one other, the woman saying, "You're a fucking bastard!" She looked a right mess, the poor soul, her skin was the colour of dirt, she had scabs on her face, on her arms, her skinny jeans were too large for her skeleton body, those same jeans were filled with holes, same as her trainers. The trainers were filthy and I could see one of her toes sticking out of the left shoe. The man looked a mess too, but not as messed up as the woman. He was walking away from her while she kept shouting at him, calling him bastard, piece of shit, and other names. I moved on, not stopping to witness more. I walked past Primark, Wilko, Holy Trinity Church, The Flying Standard pub on Trinity Street, past a few shops, and a few minutes later I was at the radio station on Victoria Street. I spent a few minutes outside, walking up and down, taking photos, looking at the pigeons, looking at the inside of a few shops from the outside, looking and wondering when I would move on with my life, as in move into a new home, get out of the area where I was living in, get a new job, finish my new novel (not this one that I'm writing but another novel), but the truth was I was working for those changes, applying for a new home, doing training at the radio, trying to learn more about what goes on behind the scenes of a radio station, promoting my work as an author at other radio stations, going for radio interviews, going to a few book events (and there was a big book event on the horizon, a few months away), and everything takes time so I would have to wait.

It was just a matter of time.

Breathe.

As always, we had a good time at the radio, learned a bit more, and I even wrote a bit of a screenplay, only 40 seconds long, more like an advert to be used for the radio, which we would record on the following week. It felt good being there (I felt good in there), at the radio, away from the outside world, kind of like being in a cocoon, separated from the madness, a few of us in one building, all different people with so many different beliefs, backgrounds, lifestyles, dreams, etc., but we were all trying to change the world for the better, bring some sort of happiness into the lives of others (and a few of us were doing a lot of voluntary work, doing mitzvahs, caring for others, praying for others without asking for a thing in return, which is what we must do). From there, after I left the radio station, I went to a building nearby, kind of like a meeting place for men, a place where people meet to talk, drink coffee and tea, eat a sandwich and a bag of crisps, maybe a piece of fruit if there's some available, all free, and when I got there I saw lots of familiar faces, people that I've known for years, people that I met at the food bank where I help out, faces that with time have become good friends (and two of those friends would soon also be getting radio training at the station that I had just left). The first person that I saw was Darius, a thirty-something-year-old man from Lithuania, a man who suffers from depression, quit drugs and alcohol a few years ago, and is now trying to start a new life, like so many of us. Darius is really tall, and he kind of reminds me of the Swedish actor Dolph Lundgren. Darius was sitting away from everyone else drinking tea and reading *The Power of Kabbalah* by Yehuda Berg. I went over to say hello to him first. I like him as a person, find him to be easy-going, quiet, and I grabbed a chair and sat next to him. We started to talk about books straight away, as we often do, and about Kabbalah, the Invisible Hand, the poison in the air, the lies (in the air and around us), and seeing that he was getting into Kabbalah I recommended a couple of books to him; *The Book of Tradition* by Abraham Ibn Daud, and *Qabbalah*, a book detailing the life and writings of Solomon ben Yehudah Ibn Gebirol. Darius wrote the names of those books down, and while he was writing I got up from my seat, went over to the counter to say hello to the two workers that prepare the sandwiches and everything else, and then I grabbed a cup of tea. Artyom, a big lad from Russia, came over to shake my hand and say hello. His English is minimal but somehow we still manage to communicate with one another. As long as people are willing to try it's always easy to communicate with others. Szymon arrived a few minutes later, followed by Piotr. They're both Polish and they're the lads who are getting radio training soon. Yakov, also from Poland, was playing pool with Habib, a young man from Pakistan. The moment he saw me, Yakov extended his arms forward and gave me a strong arm. He has really strong arms. Michal and Basile were also in the room, as was Dimi. There were more people in the room, some just browsing through the internet, and Simon was also here. Not so long ago Simon made a move on me and invited me over to his place, but I told him that's not really my thing, and once I refused his invitation he looked kind of down, demoralised, and I wondered when was the last time he had someone, but we dance differently, and we like different partners, different types of dancing, and I couldn't say yes to him. Nevertheless we have remained friends, and Simon always comes over to say hello to me. He even touched my hair when he came over to say hi, and then he asked me what I was reading and I showed him the copy of *The Outrun* by Amy Liprot which I had with me, and he told me he had listened to the latest Duran Duran album, and he had to agree with me and said that even though the album wasn't bad, it wasn't that good either; it had some good tunes but there was something missing, something from the past, that sound of Duran Duran that was slowly disappearing. I told him that I had just recently started to listen to Duran Duran again, mostly the first album and some of their B-sides, songs like *Faster than Light, Late Bar, Faith in This Colour*, and others, songs that had that distinct Duran Duran sound, or at least the sound they had when they first appeared on the scene, and I told Simon that I wasn't really into the *Rio* album, but I didn't disliked it. As a matter of fact, *Rio* contains two of my favourite Duran Duran songs; *Lonely in Your Nightmare* and *New Religion*, and *Is There Something I Should Know* is also a cracker, but I'm not a big fan of the title song, *Save a Prayer* and *Hungry Like the Wolf*, three of Duran Duran's most famous tunes, but that's just the way life is. We all have different tastes, in everything, including music and loves. It's funny how Simon has the same name as the vocalist of Duran Duran. Simon knows that I'm a big fan of Duran Duran and that I've been listening to them since I was 9-years old. I can't believe that they're still around and releasing new music.

Dimi was also in the room. I hadn't noticed him yet, but once Simon was gone Dimi came over to say hello. At first we started to talk about books, a normal chat where names like Bolaño, Eco, Saviano and others were spat out, and then, surprisingly, Dimi told me he was writing a book, a long book about his life, a book about love, divorce, revenge, and maybe even death, and that's when the conversation got really weird. I just wanted to be left alone and eat my sandwich in peace, maybe even read for a bit, be left alone for a few minutes, but it looked as if Dimi wanted to get something out of his chest, confess something, show me that he was also a detective in this insane world, a character in this simulation game, a character in the Matrix, not Neo but more like Dozer, or maybe Cypher.

Dimi is also from Poland but he doesn't hang out with Yakov, Piotr, and the other Polish lads. He's a bit of a loner, polite but distant. In 2021 I saw him quite often patrolling the streets of Coventry, always alone. Even when he comes to places like this he tends to be alone. Every once in a while he comes over to say hello to me and a few of the other lads, but he vanishes almost immediately and no one really knows that much about his life. Maybe that's a good way of living; keep your life a secret, share hardly a thing with others. Before telling me about the book he's writing he asked me what I was doing, was I writing, and if so what was I writing about, and he briefly looked at the cover of the book that I carried with me. I told him I was writing a series of books about the world right now, the madness that is occurring everywhere, the Invisible Hand's agenda to make the straight white male a minority, and the agenda is already extending towards women with women being replaced by women who used to be men (and we were witnessing that when it came to advertising beer and women sports clothes) (but the other people weren't too blame for what is happening; they're only pawns in this game called Life, and they're being used to create division), the Invisible Hand's agenda to put us all in 15-minutes prisons, the Climate Change Agenda which will stop us from travelling while the Invisible Hand and its puppets (Di Caprio, Harry Spare, Gates, and so many stars who have sold their souls to Mammon) can travel everywhere on their private jets, and Dimi was really paying attention to what I was saying, nodding every once in a while, never interrupting me, agreeing with me by nodding, and I told him that some people are so lost that they no longer know if they're male or female. Some people actually become nothing, not knowing that that's exactly what the Invisible Hand wants us to be: Nothing. And then it was Dimi's turn to talk.

By then Darius had gone outside for a cigarette. He would come back inside a few minutes later, grab a sandwich and a bag of crisps from the counter, and then he would sit outside again where he had left his cup of coffee. For a moment I thought that maybe Darius didn't want to be around Dimi that much, and that's why he decided to eat his sandwich on the back garden, but then I thought that maybe I was imagining things, seeing conspiracies where there was nothing to be seen, letting my writer's mind take the better of me, drift away like the mind of a detective, get lost in another story, a story that was only happening in my head and nowhere else. Even as a child, at school some of my friends used to say that my head was always on the clouds, or even in space, just out there, drifting away, drifting apart, taking me to other worlds, which is true, but only to a certain degree, and I'll be one of the first ones to admit that yes, as a child I tended to daydream a lot (I still do it now), but as I got older, especially in the last couple of years, I started to become more suspicious of people, and recent disappointments in love have only hardened me a bit, meaning that I'm even more suspicious now, but maybe there was no need for me to suspect Dimi of something, or even think that Darius didn't like the other man and that's why he decided to sit outside.

"It's funny you say that because I'm also writing a book about the present, and about the past, too. My past," Dimi said, looking me in the eye, showing me, by the way he looked at me, that there was more to him than I thought, something sinister, but, then again, maybe that was my writer's way of thinking and maybe I was seeing danger or doubt where there was none. But, I don't know. Something didn't look right.

"There's a lot happening in Paris right now, with the protests, people fighting the police, cars burning, and I want to go there soon and witness some of it," Dimi said, again flashing me a smile. "It's really cheap to go there by coach. You should book a trip to Paris soon, too, go and witness history in the making."

His English was minimal, or not that great, so, quite often, he would say the same thing just to make sure I was listening to him and understanding what he was saying. I told him I didn't want to go to Paris, not then, but I didn't bother to mention that I was actually thinking of going to Lourdes soon, maybe sometime in the summer, or maybe even after the summer was over, maybe in September or October, when the tickets were cheaper. As a matter of fact I had already spoken to a friend about taking a trip to Lourdes, stop in Paris for a few hours, go there by coach, on a pilgrimage with other people from the church I attend and different churches. But like I said, I didn't bother to mention this to Dimi. I no longer share that much with other people, especially my plans; there was no need to share a lot with others, not even with family members, because sometimes jealousy can be an obstacle that you must overcome. By telling Dimi about the book I was working on I was already sharing too much, but I was getting good at being cold and indifferent (I had good teachers) (thank you, bitches), and there was only so much I could share, especially with someone like Dimi since he was a stranger. Yes, he was a familiar face, a face I'd known for a couple of years, maybe longer than that, but a stranger nonetheless so why should I share my plans with him?

Not that it really mattered to Dimi whether I wanted to share details of my life with him or not. He was the one who wanted to share something (a lot) with me. More like a confession, really, something he needed to get out of his chest. From the corner of my eye I saw Yakov and Habib arguing about the game of pool they were playing; nothing new there, and I saw Szymon getting up and making his way to the reception, maybe to get a free haircut as the barber was in the building on that afternoon, and then I saw Piotr also getting up from his seat and going on the opposite direction, meaning he went to the back garden, to smoke and to chat with Darius, and while everyone was getting up and heading somewhere, Dimi was sitting in front of me, facing me, looking me in the eye, telling me silently to listen to his story, looking like Dostoevsky in the gulag, in a Siberian prison, and Dimi himself kind of reminded me of Vissarion Belinsky, who happened to be one of Fyodor's acquaintances, but I read somewhere that the writer fell out with the Russian critic, or maybe I'm dreaming it and never read about it (but I did, didn't I? How else would I know about it?), Dimi with his long parted hairstyle, Belinsky-alike, Dimi who started to tell me about his ex-wife (dumb bitches, you drive us men crazy), a bitch who slept with his then best friend (and apparently the bitch and the friend had been going at it for years), and later the bitch told Dimi she wanted the divorce, and she wanted money, and she wanted the house they were living in, and she wanted everything and couldn't care less if Dimi slept on the streets or killed himself or did whatever the fuck he wanted; the truth was she didn't give a damn about him even though, for years, he had loved her, had been faithful, worked hard for the family, and while he was doing all that the bitch was jumping up and down on someone's cock. And as if that wasn't enough, once the divorce was finalised, the bitch told Dimi that Dimi's daughter wasn't actually his but someone else's daughter, but Dimi did a DNA paternity test and his daughter is his, and while he was telling me his story I felt as if I was going through a game, as if I was actually inside a game, in a little room inside a game, someone controlling me, telling me how to react, what to do, and even what to say.

And talking about games: Habib lost the pool game because he potted the white ball after potting the black, and Yakov was laughing, and then he said, "Tough luck, my friend."

And because Habib was a good loser he shook Yakov's hand, shrugged his shoulders and then went to get himself a cup of tea from the counter. I saw him making his way along the room, looking like another character in a game, something resembling *MySims* or even that online game *Second Life*, a game I haven't played in years (and I even wrote a book called *Second Life* where one of the main characters is obsessed with *Second Life*), and a lad called James walked to the pool table, grabbed a pool cue, and then opened the game, popping two balls straight away. James then smiled and said something, and while all of this was taking place Dimi was telling me about his ex-wife and how he was still upset about it all. And who can blame him for it?

"I stopped working because of her. I told myself, I'm not giving a penny to this lying bitch," he said and I nodded because I didn't know what else to do or what to say, and I could understand his pain, I knew how he felt as I too, after I stopped living with Yu, felt like disappearing for a long time, not because I missed that snake, but then I thought about my children, and I thought about my sanity, my wellbeing, and decided to stay still, do more with my life, do a bit more for myself, just move on and let karma do the rest. The radio was playing some crap music. To make it worse someone turned the volume up. A song called *Death* by the Preoccupations came to my mind just then. I hadn't heard them in ages (where they still around?). Or Icehouse. Or Duran Duran. Right then, after that song came to my head, followed by another bunch of songs by various artists, I felt like going home to burn a CD to listen in the car, but that wouldn't be possible until later in the evening because, from there, I would have to go to Yu's place and see my children, and then take Leaf home with me as we were spending some family time together, watch a movie, eat popcorn, maybe grab something to eat from McDonald's on the way back to my place.

Dimi told me that his ex-wife was no longer living with his former friend. In fact his friend had moved to Paris in 2021. From what Dimi told me the other man had a good job in Paris and I was wondering if that was one of the reasons why Dimi wanted to visit France. He showed me a small video camera which he carried with him and told me he wanted to start making small videos of the world, record things around him, kind of like a long documentary, something to pass the time, and I said, "Go for it. That sounds like a great idea. I too, every once in a while, record small videos with my mobile phone, and later I post it on YouTube."

"You have a YouTube channel?" he asked, leaning forward, his dark eyes almost entering me. Or at least it felt like that.

I nodded and told him a bit about my YouTube channel, and his face went really stiff, the eyes becoming even more penetrating, or something like that, and he smiled and said, "Yes, I think I might need to start my own channel, too."

"Yeah, you should," I said the first thing that came to mind, and then I diverted my eyes from his and looked around the room. James was now playing pool with Albert, a local lad who also comes here every once in a while, and Yakov was talking to Darius, who by now was sitting inside the room and not in the back garden. Basile had just grabbed a sandwich and a bag of crisps from the counter and sat in a corner on his own, earphones on, and I watched him take a big bite of the sandwich.

"I want to go to Paris soon," Dimi said and I turned my attention to him. "I want to record the protests, and I also want to pay a visit to the son of a bitch that slept with my ex."

His face was becoming aggressive, and his eyes seemed to grow even darker, which wasn't possible (unless the creators of this game called *Life* decided to make his character scarier). I saw then, too late I must add, that Dimi was slightly mad, or maybe mad is the wrong way to put it. He was upset. Angry with the world. Angry with what Life had given him. A few years ago, in 2020, I had been there too; angry with the world, angry with certain people, and after Ellie broke up with me I also felt that way, and it was then, after that latest breakup, that I decided to go a bit cold, become a bit indifferent, stop always being the nice guy. When some old acquaintances (I will no longer call them friends) messaged me asking me for favours after ignoring me for two years or more, I quickly told them I couldn't help them. I even felt like asking, "Where the hell were you when I was going through the darkness? Why didn't you say a word?" but that would have been a waste of time.

Thanks to meditation and with the help of some friends that I have made, and thanks to faith and the belief that a Great Power could restore me back to sanity, I managed to leave the anger behind, but I also know that something inside me has changed and that I can't – and don't want to- go back to that person I used to be. Dimi still has that anger inside him, the anger of being hurt, anger that comes with injustice and unfairness, and he tells me that after his divorce, when he was already alone, living in a small room, he used to go out and let his anger out by getting into fights. Looking back, I actually remember seeing him a couple of times with bruises on his face, a black eye, and one time he even had his right hand bandaged. And didn't someone bit his ear once? Who did he fight? Mike Tyson?

"Sooner or later you will have to move on, forget about the divorce and the anger, and let karma deal with your ex and her ex-partner," I said.

Dimi smiled, and in that smile I saw the anger, and I saw that he was lost, still trying to find his way out of the darkness, but instead of looking up so he could see the light (and a way out of the darkness) he was looking further down, into the darkness, digging his way down, smiling at the darkness while he slid down, smiling uncontrollably, a desperate smile, a smile that wasn't really a smile but a cry for help, and later that night, when I was already in bed, sleeping like a baby, lost in a dream, or trying to find my way out of that dream (WAKE UP!), I saw myself standing outside a cave, a dark cave, a cave made out of a woman's hair and not of rocks, and I saw a face inside that cave, a tiny face that was being pulled into the darkness, a smiling face, and I realised it was the face of Dimi, and in my dream he said, "Help me," before being pulled into the darkness. I wanted to go after him, do something for him, help him, but the cave started to shut on him and I started to back away, watching the cave turn to nothing, the clouds above me slowly dispersing, the blue sky turning red, and then a snake crawled from the bushes (where the hell was I?) and I saw the snake heading towards me, moving at a slow speed, moving at the speed of a snail, and even though the snake was taking its time I found myself unable to move, and even though I was dreaming (and I think I knew I was dreaming) I was really scared, panicking, and then someone grabbed me from behind and said, "Come."

I turned around and saw Ellie. My Ellie. My Ellie that was never mine.

"What are you doing here?" I thought but didn't say a word to her. "I'm trying to forget you."

Ellie smiled. And then she led me away, towards another part of the garden, or whatever the hell we were. I didn't even bother to look back to see if the snake was following us or not.

I don't know what else happened in the dream. I can't remember. Maybe that was the end of the dream.

Dimi kept on talking. The darkness kept on growing. He was lost in the darkness, lost in the anger of the past, his insides being consumed by revenge.

Revenge is a disease.

Revenge is reproduced by the hate that you carry inside yourself and Dimi had a lot of hate inside himself. And that hate was slowly consuming him from within, eating his insides. And then I saw that the hate he carried inside him was the cave that I would later see in my dream, a cave that was a woman, a hate that was his ex-woman, a hate that he would have to let go of if he wanted a new start in life.

"I want to go to Paris not only to see the protests and record it all but also to visit that motherfucker who slept with my ex-wife, and I want to torch his car. With so many cars burning in Paris who will miss one more?" Dimi said, and I knew (and saw) that he was serious about it and that he would most likely go ahead with his plan, a plan that was insane, or maybe just plain bad. The actual plan itself wasn't bad (and Dimi could actually get away with it) but the action itself would be bad.

Again I told him, "Just forget about it, Dimi. Karma will deal with them."

But what was I saying?

Dimi had a perfect plan, or 90% perfect, maybe 89% (What could go wrong? Everything!), but who else knew of his plan? Only me or had he told others about it? I wouldn't open my mouth and reveal his crazy plan to others and he knew that, but had he told others about it? And could they keep their mouths shut? But then I remembered that Dimi was a loner so there was the slight chance that I was the only person who knew of his plan.

"No. I don't want for karma to deal with that piece of shit. I'll be his karma," Dimi said. I was totally against it but Dimi couldn't care less. Anyway, I didn't even say that I was against it because I knew there was no point in saying that much about it.

He knew I'd gone through a breakup, followed by a divorce during lockdown, and he knew about my fight with depression and my flight from the darkness, so maybe he thought of me as some sort of an ally, even a silent accomplice, and because I wrote books and stories and he was just beginning as a writer, or maybe he'd always been a writer but only wrote stories in his head until recently, never bothering to put the words into paper, not until he'd gone through a painful divorce and all sorts of pain, and writing about your pain can be like some sort of therapy, anyway, since we were both writers, divorced writers, and since we had both survived the darkness (but I had a feeling that Dimi was still navigating through the darkness, not really making his way out of it, not yet, not then, navigating slowly through it, kind of stuck in it, so maybe he wasn't even navigating through the darkness; maybe he was just stuck in it, looking to the sides —and up and down, being driven by the anger, but anger is blind and instead of leading you towards the exit and the light, the anger leaves you stuck in the darkness, and sooner or later you'll have to let go of the anger, just let go or else you'll sink —and die- in the darkness) Dimi probably thought of me as a friend, at the least someone he could confide in, a confidant, but the more he told me about his forthcoming trip to Paris the more I saw that he actually needed —wanted- a friend, a real friend, even an accomplice, someone to tell him that his plan would work out and that he was right and should go ahead with it. I told him again to forget about it, just let it go, let life and karma and a Higher Power deal with those who had hurt him but he was having none of it.

"Sooner or later, without you even knowing it, those who sneer and lie will fade and die, and they will die with regrets, carrying a heavy load on their backs, and you must forget, forgive and move on, and I know that these are hard things to do, especially when it comes to forgiveness, but, if we want to be forgiven for our own mistakes, we too must learn how to forgive others, even if they have caused us a lot of pain, and at the same time we must discard of them, leave then behind," I said but he wasn't registering a word of what I was saying.

Habib went back to the counter and grabbed himself another cup of tea and a banana. Basile was now playing pool with Darius. Basile was such a bad player it was almost painful to watch him play. He would grab the pool cue and then just completely miss the white ball, but no one would say a thing about it. In fact other players would even give him tips on how to be a better player but Basile never seemed to listen to anyone.

By now, thankfully, Dimi had stopped talking about his ex-wife, revenge, burning cars, and he showed me how his small video camera worked. I was listening to him but at the same time my body was shutting down. I was so tired, which came as no surprise seeing that I had finished a 12-hour shift, gone home, got changed, and then went straight to the radio station for training. And I still had to get my daughter from school and then drop her at her mother's house. On Tuesdays either her or her brother would usually stay with me but I was too tired on that day to have any of them staying with me and I needed to get a lot of sleep without having to worry about getting up early on the following day. My poor body (and my heart) needed the rest, plenty of it, or else I would shut down permanently.

Dimi was still talking and I was partially listening to him, missing a few words of what he was saying, sometimes not really understanding some of what he was saying. After a while he either realised that I was tired or that I wasn't paying full attention to what he was saying, or both, or he was tired himself, so he got up and told me he was going home to write. We shook hands and I told him I would be going home soon too, which was a bit of a lie because I was going to Earlsdon first to get my daughter, and then I would have to drop her at my ex-wife's home. A few minutes later after Dimi had left, I left, too.

I made my way towards Earlsdon, my body feeling a bit tired. I looked at my watch; a few minutes past 2pm. I felt good, or sort of good: there were a few things missing in my life but I had to stop complaining and just move on, and I walked at an easy pace, the talk with Dimi still playing in my head, playing on repeated mode, and I felt like laughing even though it was no laughing matter. But what else could I do apart from laughing it off?

I crossed the road, saw a couple of women stepping out of a gym on Upper Well Street, fit women, both of them wore leggings and hoodies and colourful trainers. I made my way down Belgrade Plaza, saw a young Chinese woman talking on the phone just outside Pizza Express, a really pretty woman, too young for me, and I let out a long sigh and smiled. My ex-wife Yu briefly came to mind. I remember when I first met her, in London, February 2005. I thought then she would be my eternal wife, the only woman I would love for the rest of my life, but I was wrong, so damn wrong, but that's the way life goes and I just have to move on. I'm not the only person to have gone through a breakup, a divorce, I'm not the only writer who has travelled through the Dark Night of the Soul and thought about suicide, not even the only writer who has gone through a lockdown, or a breakup during a lockdown while the world was being affected by a virus, and I'm sure there were others like me who wasted so many tears while sitting inside their cars or standing outside churches. But life goes on and I'm glad I'm still here. My friend Lee, who's also an author, gave me a push towards a new life when he got me in touch with his publisher, and then I met Ellie and a few other people, and I saw that life could still be beautiful. You lose some people and you gain others, and a lot of the time you lose those you don't need or people who stopped loving you or never loved you and afterwards life brings more beauty into your life. I met a lot of beautiful souls during the years of 2020-2022, especially those whom I work with at the food bank, and they have given me strength to carry on. Then there are my friends Santiago, Ariel, and even Cassio who have also been a good shoulder to cry on, not to mention Cassandra and Gary. And the people I have met at the church in Kingsland Avenue. Life goes on. I tried to tell this to Dimi but I guess he needs to go through his own pain. I just hope he doesn't do anything silly. And if life hadn't given me a divorce and later the breakup with Ellie, I wouldn't have written these three books that I wrote. The writer needed inspiration so Life said, "There you go. Here's love, heartbreak and pain. Write about this, fool."

I kept on walking, walked past the Quakers on Hill Street, took a right turn, went up Hill Street, as if I were heading towards Barras Lane, then took a left, walked past the Urban Village, which is student accommodation, built in the last few years, and I made my way towards the Spon End subway through a backstreet, Al Kooper's *Baby, Please Don't Go* playing on my earphones, a bit of cold wind in the air, sunshine too, and even though I was tired I was also happy because soon I would be seeing my children. I needed more than a few minutes with them every few days or so, a bit more, maybe a lot more, but they were nearby, only a few minutes' drive from where I lived, so I also knew I was lucky for that. I was a few steps away from the subway when I saw a woman crouching down against a corner. It took me a few minutes to realise that she was taking a dump on a public space in the middle of the afternoon. She was lost to the darkness, a different type of darkness where Dimi lived in. I more or less knew who that woman was. Every once in a while she would come to the food bank to get some food and something to drink, sometimes she would even ask for some clothes, but every time I saw her she was always dressed in rags. Someone once told me she was lost to heavy drugs, the worse type of drugs, but she'd once been a gorgeous woman. The beauty she once had was now completely gone but I'd seen other people getting their inner and outer beauty back even though they had also been lost to drugs. But to get that beauty back those people had to turn to Jesus for help. They had to leave their old lives behind and dedicate themselves to the Son.

The woman saw me too and she started to shout at me, saying, "What the fuck are you looking at? You bastard!!! Get out of here, you bastard!!!"

I didn't stop. There was nothing to see, nothing but a disgusting sight, but I wasn't blaming the poor woman for it. She was lost in her own personal hell and it would take a lot of strength for her to get away from it. Later, once I was already in Earlsdon, I thought, "How the hell did she clean her bum? Did she have some toilet paper with her?"

After swearing at me, she said, "I'm sorry. I'm so sorry. I'm so sorry."

The shouting became almost like a plea for mercy and forgiveness but who was she talking to? Me? A Higher Power?

I heard her sobbing, I kid you not, but I didn't stop to look behind me. If anything, I hurried my pace. Even if I wanted I couldn't help that woman. Sure, I could have stopped and maybe listen to her, maybe try to say a kind word, but not then, not on the spot where she had just taken a dump, not in the state she was.

I went down the subway, up the subway, walked past the Meadow House on Meadow Street, saw a familiar face standing outside Meadow House, smoking a cigarette, a man whose name I'd forgotten; I first met him in 2020, by Langar Aid House. He waved at me and I waved back. He didn't do a thing with his life; didn't work, didn't exercised, read a few books from the library or books that friends gave him, spent his money on cigarettes and alcohol, and he got all his food from food banks and donations. Meanwhile, there I was, dead-tired from a 12-hour night-shift and a few hours of training at a radio station; and I still had a father's duties to do. Again, I let out a long sight. Sooner or later I would have to quit that night job and find myself a job with decent hours.

On that same night, before heading to bed, I quickly read the news online and read somewhere that Steven Seagal was teaching martial arts to troops in Russia. Once I went through the whole article I thought to myself, "We're really living in a simulated reality, or in a game, and its creators are having a laugh. Let's see how the game ends."

I glanced down, just to check the time on the laptop, saw that it was getting late, and I was so tired. Nevertheless I quickly logged on and went to the Awakened Page just to browse through the news. There was a lot of talk about Chat GPT AI, Artificial Intelligence, the end of the world, how AI creators are playing with fire, and the usual doomsday talk.

There was also a lot of talk about people changing their sexes, becoming someone/something else, the pushing of the Agenda that would allow children of any age to change their sex, an Agenda that was not only wrong but even evil and devious. A child can't make such a drastic decision. That Agenda itself was a sign of cultural collapse, but if anyone went against it and decided to protect the children they would actually be persecuted. Past writers who were no longer with us were being persecuted by things they wrote decades ago, even centuries ago. The world was upside down, slowly collapsing. And the machine, yes. Someone wrote in one of the comments that Artificial Intelligence is actually an outer dimensional entity, but then someone else wrote something that was both scary and made sense. He wrote that Artificial Intelligence is actually the image of the Beast in the Bible, writing a verse of the Bible on his comment.

Revelation 13:15

And he had power to give life unto the image of the beast, that the image of the beast should both speak, and cause that as many as would not worship the image of the beast should be killed.

I took a deep breath.

I wanted to go to sleep and at the same time I wanted to go through every single comment on that post about Artificial Intelligence and the Beast.

Someone else wrote that some machine had already outsmarted its creators and that the Machine could communicate with spirits and demons. This person said that the smart thing to do would be to shut

Artificial Intelligence down for good because we're playing with fire. Not so long ago Elon Musk and other people signed a letter where they urged Artificial Intelligence labs to pause AI development, and someone else said that pausing the development of the Machine isn't enough. We actually need to shut it down for good. Forever. But that won't happen. The geeks in the room will fight amongst themselves and with their egos to see who will create the better machine, not knowing that they're actually opening Pandora's Box. And once this box is open it will be a long time before anyone can close it. But what can I, a literally poor writer, do about and against the Machine?

I believe that, in the end, the Machine will be the only thing that can bring an end to the Invisible Hand but will anyone be able to defeat the Machine?

What about the Star People?

Or the Naga Lokas?

Can they do something about the Machine?

The Time Traveller told me that the Naga Lokas don't want to be around Artificial Intelligence and intelligent machines because it has no control over it.

What about the Star People?

Who are they?

Native American tribes speak of astral beings who visited them in the past and even shared some of their knowledge with the tribes, and an ancient Hopi Tribe legend talks about a race of Star People who were either our ancestors or creators, and they will return one day to restore balance to our planet, a planet that is actually theirs or was created by them or their Creator. And is their Creator our Creator? But what if they have forgotten about us and moved on? As for the Naga Lokas, they're too busy in their own world, living in another dimension, and they will probably just watch us all destroy one another and destroy the Machine, and only then will they resurface. Crazy, yes, I know, but, bloody hell, Hollywood action man Steven Seagal is training Russian troops. It doesn't get any crazier than that, does it?

I finally turned the laptop off, a few minutes after 9pm, and after saying my prayers I went straight to bed. I must have fallen asleep straight away and later I dreamt of Dimi and the cave. And Ellie. But Ellie was only briefly in my dream.

Sometime during the night, after the first dream was over, I woke up with an erection, which was nothing new. I needed to pee but instead of going downstairs to use the bathroom I went back to sleep. I was still tired and my body was telling me to rest, go back to sleep, pee later. Almost straight away, once I had fallen asleep, I found myself in another dream, lying in a bed, not my bed, that is to say not the bed I was sleeping in but another bed, probably a bed the same size as the bed I was sleeping in, in the bedroom I was renting, a large bed with clean white blankets on top of me. I felt a hand on my back, playing with my spine, running along my spine, feeling the bones on my back. I opened my eyes, but only in my dream because I was still sleeping, and I saw Ellie lying next to me, gazing at me with her blue eyes; and her eyes were piercing through me. Or at least it felt that way. Her long strong fingers were now on my stomach and I saw that she was naked. And so was I – but only in the dream. She kept looking at me, smiling, silently telling me that everything was going to be okay and that we were going to have sex. And then I saw her thin body on top of me, her almost hairless vagina rubbing against my penis (and by then I really needed to pee) (and my brain was telling me to wake up and go to the bathroom), and then she slid down my penis, always smiling, smiling while riding my penis which was now in desperate need to let it all out. The ceiling was painted white, the ceiling of the room we were in; I don't know why I remember that but I do, with a few flowers on it, white flowers, and I realised that we were in a bedroom that I'd never seen, a copy of a novel by Proust on top of a bedside table. The book was *Finding Time Again*, the last volume of *In Search of Lost Time*. For some reason I thought we were in Paris, and then, don't ask me how, I knew for sure that we were in Paris. I was about to come, or about to pee in bed. I opened my eyes and Ellie was gone, I was back in Coventry, or still in Coventry I should say, and I still needed to pee. With that in mind I quickly rushed downstairs so I could use the bathroom. Part of me wanted to masturbate, let it all out, but I fought that desire. And what did the dream meant? Maybe nothing.

Whenever I was awake I was no longer thinking that much of Ellie, but every once in a while she would still visit me in my dreams. But not that often. As for the fact we were in Paris, maybe I was only dreaming of that city because of what Dimi had told me earlier on.

Since I was already up, after saying my prayers I had breakfast, showered, got changed, and afterwards I went for a long walk. I took a notebook with me. I wanted to sit somewhere and write.

When I stepped out of the house I saw that it was a good day; not too hot but not too cold either, and instead of going straight to the city centre I decided to quickly go to church and pray the Rosary. From there I would make my way to the city centre, grab a hot chocolate from Greggs, and then go to Central Library, sit down, and write. I could have gone to Earlsdon but I wanted a change of airs, put my mind and body somewhere else, slowly leave the past behind, erase old memories and old loves and create a new history. I was cured from the heartbreak.

Finally!!!

Halleluiah!!!

I never thought I would say this but I could even see myself living far away from where I was living, live somewhere else, start again, as soon as possible, love someone else, be loved and respected - love and respect: things I felt were missing from my last relationship and even from my broken marriage. I felt as if I was finally coming out of the dark, completely out of it, and I could feel the changes in me, changes that I never thought were possible. In a way, because she had broken up with me, I felt a bit of gratitude towards Ellie. Even Yu. I had gone cold, only a tiny bit, but I needed that coldness inside me. The coldness had become a shield, some sort of protection for the next relationship.

Because of the coldness, or maybe thanks to it, I was no longer in a rush to get involved with someone else. I was putting myself first, at last, me, my children and my dreams. Everyone else would have to wait. I had offered my true love to some people but they ignored it, ignored me, and then dumped me, just put me aside as if I was a piece of garbage, but I was coming to terms with it all; sometimes, while reliving the past and my needy actions, I would even laugh about it; what else could I do? Cry about it? Go back to the depression? Chase someone who didn't want to be with me? I'd done all of that and it took me nowhere. It was time to try something new, do things in a different way.

Instead of walking all the way to Kingsland Avenue I drove there. I had a few hours to spare before I had to get my daughter from school but I wanted to use some of that time to write and not to be rushing around, so even though I wanted to go for a long walk I decided to drive first to church, and after saying my prayers I drove to Barras Lane where I parked my car.

I thought about visiting my friend Saul who lived nearby, but he was working from home and I didn't want to disturb him plus I wanted to get some work done on my new novel. The truth was my new novel had been left behind for a long time, almost forgotten, because I'd been too busy with radio training, not to mention I'd been so busy writing about heartbreak, new beginnings, and damn bitches that had broken my heart. I was using a lot of bad language, just letting my anger out, that little bit of anger I had still left in me, but I also knew that I would have to change my speech. I was never a person who used bad language but as I wrote about all those who had hurt me and let me down, I really felt like cursing to the skies. But what would have been the point of it?

I grabbed my laptop bag and then made my way to the library, but first I stopped by Ed's Café, situated inside the Coventry Market, grabbed myself a cup of coffee for £1.20, a bargain when you think about it (and the coffee from Ed's Café is really good) (I decided to go there instead of Greggs), took a short walk along the market, looked at some old books, bought nothing, and from there I made my way to the library. When I was stepping out of the Market, by the exit that leads to the Tesco Express on Market Way, I saw a young woman looking at me, her eyes following me as I walked out of the market. She wore a long grey coat, dark trousers, an orange top, and white trainers. Her face looked vaguely familiar but I wasn't really staring at her; I was only looking sideways so I couldn't really tell who she was. I took a left turn by the Max Mobility Centre, felt those eyes still on me, the eyes of the woman whom I thought I vaguely knew, and then I saw someone else that I also vaguely know stepping out of Superdrug but she didn't see me and I didn't bother to say hi. I walked past Sports Direct and briefly thought about going inside because I needed a new pair of trainers; Converse All Stars, of course, because those are the only shoes that I buy nowadays although things might change later on. More than once I bought different trainers but somehow I never got used to them so now I only buy Converse trainers. In the end I chose not to go inside Sports Direct and kept on walking but when I looked behind me I saw that the woman from the market was walking behind me, not too far from where I was and getting closer, and she was still staring at me. And then I saw that the woman was Charlie's daughter but instead of waiting for her to get close to me I kept on walking. Maybe she wasn't even following me. She had two blue plastic bags with her so I assumed she'd gone to the market to buy a few things and was now heading home. I hurried my pace just a tiny bit. I didn't want to make it too obvious that I was trying to get away from her but I also didn't want to wait around and see if she would come and talk to me. But why would she? It wasn't as if we knew one another. I'd seen her with Charlie a few times but we'd never been introduced.

I entered the library and went up the steps. Out of the corner of my eye I saw that Charlie's daughter was only a few steps behind me.

"What the hell is going on?" I thought.

Unless I ran and hide, it was almost impossible to ignore the situation, but was she even following me or coming to see me? I took a deep breath and decided to let the situation play itself. Instead of hurrying my pace I slowed down but didn't stop. I made my way towards a quiet corner, sat down, and was about to reach for one of my Muji notebooks when Charlie's daughter stopped in front of me.

"Hi," she said.

I nodded and replied with another hi.

She put the plastic bags down, pulled up a chair, and sat next to me.

"You're the Writer, yes?" she asked.

 "I'm a writer, yes," I replied.

"You're friends with my mum," she said and I nodded. I loved the way she said mum. It was caring, adorable, and it showed me that she was really close to her mother.

"She has a few books of yours at home. I've seen you a few times in Earlsdon and mum said you were a writer and that she was friends with you."

I didn't know what to say. I had come to the library to write but I could see that I wouldn't be writing for a while. And what did Charlie's daughter want from me?

Just then Darius walked past our table. He gently nodded when he saw me and I nodded back. He went upstairs, to where the computers are, but I knew he wouldn't be using a computer. He would probably just use his mobile phone to watch something or he would probably browse through some books.

"Are you close to my mum?" Charlie's daughter asked.

What did she mean with that?

Close how?

Did she think I was having some sort of affair or relationship with her mother?

"Were just friends," I said which was true. I didn't even bother to tell her that I hardly knew her mother. I'd spoken to Charlie a few times but how well did I know her?

The daughter didn't say a word for the next few seconds (and what intolerable seconds they were). She just sat there looking at me. I liked her face but I also realised that I preferred Charlie's face. The daughter was as pretty as the mother, but the mother had something about her that made her face more interesting. Anyway, none of it really mattered because I didn't see myself getting involved romantically with any of them. My heart was slowly rebuilding itself, putting a protective layer around it, telling me (and my brain) that it was time to become a bit colder when it came to relationships, or more protective, guarded, cautious, and stop the damn neediness. I was dead. Or the old me was dead, at least when it came to relationships. I had endured so much pain in the last three years that now my heart was taking control of things, or was mutating into a new heart, communicating more with the brain, telling me (and my dick) to slow down, take it easy, don't be so eager to love and then don't be surprised when the other person turns out to be a disappointment.

I wanted to laugh.

I wanted to get up from my seat and shout, "HALLELUIAH!"

And then I would take Charlie's daughter into a backroom, fuck her in the ass, and afterwards say to her, "Let's just be friends."

I saw then that I was losing the plot, walking away from what I was learning at church, walking away from what really mattered.

I would have to leave the bad language behind, leave all that didn't matter behind.

I couldn't let disappointment and heartbreak to shape me into something else, someone else, someone that differed from the Son. The goal was to become someone better, a better person, a better father, a better son. Better. I knew then I would have to leave the bad language behind once and for all.

Charlie's daughter introduced herself.

"I'm Amanda," she said.

"I'm M÷," I said.

"I know."

She told me her mother had a couple of my books at home and Amanda had just started reading *dUst*, my first novel, published in 2021.

And then she went quiet. Again. She looked as if she had a lot on her mind, maybe stuff concerning me and her mother, suspicions about our relationship, but Charlie and I were just friends, nothing but friends.

"Are you sleeping with my mum?" she finally asked the question that had been eating her inside.

I wasn't at all surprised by that question and didn't even try to fake a surprised look.

"No. We're just friends; that's all. As a matter of fact we met here, at this library, by letter R, where some of my books are," I said. "And I don't really know Charlie that well."

I didn't know what else to say apart from the truth. And why even lie about it when there was no need for it?

I took my glasses off and laid them on top of Joël Dicker's new book, *The Enigma of Room 622*. I only need the glasses for driving and to see far away, but I can read, type and write without the glasses on, and then I sat there, silently staring at Amanda who was also not saying a word, and I wondered for how long the silence would go on, who would say the next word, and I was starting to get a bit annoyed because I had gone to the library to write, not to waste my time staring at a young woman who thought I was sleeping with her mother, but even though I was annoyed the writer in me was saying, "Write about this moment. Write about everything."

Just like that, thanks to the writer inside me, the little anger I felt suddenly became a joke, something to laugh about, a boring story that I would have to write, and I knew I would write about it even if it was silly. I would write about it even if no one read it for a long time, I would write it and publish it, knowing that one day someone would probably read these books of mine and then that same person would also write about his own life, or her own life, and some of their books would then replace some of my books on the shelves of some libraries, or in one of their Kindles or whatever objects people will one day use to read books. But I could also see a world without books, a world that wasn't that distant, a world where people would burn books just so they –the people- could keep warm. What a sad world that would be; a picture of both the past and the future. And one day the present would become the past and the past would become the future. We were living in a simulated reality, a game that kept going back and forth in time, a game of two halves: past and present, nothing else beyond it: the future was a mirage, the future was the past, the future was a joke, and the Invisible Hand probably knew about it. No wonder they were so greedy; they wanted to enjoy the present before going back to the past. The Time Traveller was a joke. Or a joker. Or maybe the joke was on all of us.

Looking over Amanda's shoulder I saw a woman approaching us in the distance, a woman who, from far away (and maybe because I didn't have my glasses on), kind of reminded me of Ellie, and in that moment I felt as if an invisible hand (sigh) was squeezing my heart, letting me know that I still hadn't forgotten the woman I had last loved which made no sense (but does love even make sense?) because Ellie's mind had never been in the relationship and in the end she just let me go so easily, so coldly, throwing me away like a piece of clothing that she couldn't bear to see in front of her. And while she moved on so easily from our relationship and was living and loving and laughing, I still felt a bit of longing for her non-existential love.

"What an idiot," I thought, addressing me as the idiot, thinking that maybe I should have gone to Charlie's house when I had the chance and then go down on her while she slapped my face. And then I smiled and even let out a little laugh because my thoughts were becoming like a bad comedy. By then the woman I thought was Ellie had already walked past us; and no, it wasn't Ellie but she did look a bit like her, and Amanda was giving me funny looks, probably wondering if I was crazy or high, and not wanting for her to think I was either (but to be honest I couldn't care less what she thought of me), I told her I was thinking about a movie I'd seen on the previous night, which was a lie because I hadn't seen a movie in ages, and I mentioned the movie *Fletch* with Chevy Chase because that was the first movie that came to mind, and asked her if she had seen that movie and she said no.

"But you know who Chevy Chase is, don't you?" I asked.

She nodded, adding afterwards, "He was in the Community series."

"I didn't watch that," I said.

Time was flying by and I wanted to write a bit, catch up on my new novel, which wasn't so new because I'd been working on it for the last couple of years, on and off really because I wrote a few other books while working on that novel too, and I also wanted to write about that encounter with Amanda, and about a few other events, but it looked as if she wasn't in a rush to leave and I couldn't just get up and go somewhere else, or ignore her and just start writing. If a person wants to be practical about everything, of course I could just ignore her, or get up and go somewhere else, but that's not how life works. Or at least that's not how I do things, no matter how much I've changed in the last few months.

The woman I had briefly mistaken for Ellie walked past us and I noticed she had a couple of books with her. One of the books was a copy of *Our Endless Numbered Days* but I couldn't see what else she had picked up from the library shelves. In fact I'm not even sure if she had picked up those books from the shelves or if she had them with her when she came into the library. And just as that last thought was floating through my head Amanda said, "I would love for my parents to get back together."

I looked at her and in the space of a second she became a little girl; a child who wanted to see her parents get back together, and I too became a little child but only temporarily, a lost child, or kind of lost, not only lost but sad, too, a child who had never seen his parents together, and now my children were going through the same thing, living without their parents in the same room, in the same house, living without me.

It was a time of confession, a time of confiding, a time of asking, but who was listening to us?

"I never saw my parents together. They got divorced when I was a baby. My marriage broke up in 2020 and I haven't lived with my children since then," I said.

For a moment or two I thought I was about to cry and the thought of crying in front of a stranger petrified me. I also realised I was sick of crying. I had spent years crying, especially the last few years, and I no longer wanted to cry. The sadness was still there, still present, inside me, but I wanted to move away from it, create a new life, forge a new path, search for happiness and not spend my entire life lost in the sadness.

For the next few minutes me and Amanda became two kids, two little children with adult bodies and childish hearts, two little children who were searching for something, for that evasive thing called a happy family that stays together.

I had come to the library to write and to forget the sadness, but the sadness followed me there only to tell me that it wanted for its parents to get back together. The sadness was staring at me with her little blue eyes, maybe expecting me to say something. So many people come to me to tell me about their problems and I always wonder why I seem to attract them to me? What is it about me or my face that makes people open up to me?

"Does your father want to get back together with your mother?" I asked.

The writer in me could picture beings from another dimension watching us while listening to Klaus Schulze's *Bayreuth Return*, the Naga Lokas hiding from the Machine while watching the human race slowly destroy itself, but the only people that were looking at us were a few workers who were pushing trolleys filled with books and CDs or people who would walk past us, and I looked at my watch and saw that time was really running fast past me and soon, without me even being aware of it, I wouldn't have much time left to write, read, and just unwind, but the writer was telling me that Amanda was more important than whatever I wanted to read because she was a part of my story, a minor character in that book of mine that seemed to go nowhere, a book that was already on its third volume (this is it: the third –and last- volume – will there be more?), and even though I wanted to write this book, at the same time I wanted to stop writing this type of story and go back to science-fiction, real science-fiction and not this badly disguised novels which I imply are sci-fi but they're actually real stuff and if you do your research you will be scared by what you find and you will see that not only is the news fake, history itself is also fake. And then what? What will you do with that knowledge? How can you close your eyes (and your mind) and go back to being the sheep you used to be?

"Yes, he does, but mum isn't in a rush to get back together with him. I don't even know if she wants to get back with him," she said.

A couple of students walked past us. I heard them mentioning a boy's name, saying he was gross. They went upstairs, to where the computers are. Seconds later, two men in their mid-thirties also made their way upstairs. I wondered then how many writers were in there, at the library, writers and poets, and what were they working on?

"This is none of my business but why did they get divorced?" I asked.

Amanda shrugged her shoulders.

"They both have strong tempers, different opinions, and one day; I don't know how or why, father just moved away, at first giving the excuse that he was going to work in another city, and the days soon turned into weeks and mum knew he wasn't coming back. I guess they just drifted apart. I was too busy with my studies and my own life to even notice that my parents were living different lives. One morning I came to see mum and was told that she and father had gotten divorced," she said.

She told me later that her parents had gotten divorced in 2019 but that they had been living apart a couple of years prior to that.

It was quiet at the library and I saw a few familiar faces walking past the table where I was chatting with Amanda and they would greet me with me a nod. I would nod back, sometimes greet them with a good morning, and after a while Amanda said, "You seem to know a lot of people in Coventry."

I told her that when the lockdown of 2020 started instead of staying home like told by the government I went out every single day for long walks, met hundreds of people, and even started helping out at a food bank so I wouldn't go insane, and I told her that a lot of the people who had just walked past us went to the food bank to be fed and we all became friends.

"You're a bit of a rebel. Instead of obeying the curfew you went the opposite way," she said.

"Hey, Boris and Keir were having parties, Hancock was cheating on his wife, Cummings was travelling around the country to see his family even though he had symptoms of the Invisible Enemy, and we were told we couldn't go anywhere and meet other people? What a farce. These idiots make idiotic laws without having any concern for the people and then make fun of us and their own laws while enjoying rich lifestyles paid by our taxpayers' money," I said.

The writer was back. He was speaking for me. He was telling Amanda and the world how everything really works and that our leaders, no matter what party is in power, don't give a damn about us. And he –I- would write about it because that's what writers do. Or some do. The truth is we're living at a time where many people are afraid to write the truth, or to write what they really want to write, and a lot of straight white men aren't even published by major publishers or accepted by agents. It's ridiculous. More concerning, or equally concerning, is the fact we can't even say what a woman really is. Nowadays, in this confusing age, everyone can be anyone and anything (or so the lying media tells you), but that's not how life and science work. But even science has been bought and is now manipulated by the Invisible Hand. I was saying all this to Amanda; it was my turn to talk and I had a bit to say, and Amanda just sat there. It was her turn to listen and nod. I told her that the people were being manipulated by lies printed by the press and spoken by our leaders.

"But the real leaders are invisible," I said. "They speak from behind the scenes. They fly around the world along with their puppets who disguise themselves as princes and movie stars but they're all charlatan and liars. They preach about the climate change while flying around the world on their private jets. It's all a joke and the joke's on us."

"You sound like my father," Amanda said.

A teenager walked past us, face mask on, a snowflake trying not to melt, glued to his mobile phone, glued to the lie, head down, afraid of oxygen, afraid of fresh air, afraid of people because he, or whatever the hell he identified with, was swallowing the lie that was being fed to him by the machine. Maybe some people were right. Maybe the machine (the mobile phone, the computer, the machines that were yet to arrive, Artificial Intelligence, etc.) was the beast, and most of the world carried the beast with them. We were connected to the machine (connected to the beast?) but disconnected from the human race. The writer wanted to be left alone. He had notes to write, craziness to let out. Later that night, when I went to bed, after falling asleep, I saw myself as a machine-free writer walking along a semi-bright corridor, an illuminated floor in front of me. I was carrying a typewriter with me, an Olivetti Lettera 22 1961 portable typewriter, and I was following a man who wore a long white robe and sandals. He had long hair and a short beard, and I thought, "He's either the Son or a hippie."

I saw a few doors to my right and to my left, and I saw what looked like floating cages or floating phone boxes (and *Doctor Who* came to mind just then), but I stayed behind the man with the white robe, and when he got to the end of the corridor he opened a door and went in. I followed him, and seconds later I found myself inside the biggest library I had ever seen, tens and tens of floors of books, so many books that I felt a bit dizzy. The man with the white robe was no longer on sight and I wondered where he had gone, but then something inside me kind of showed me the way; it was just a feeling pushing me forward, telling me where to go, and I followed that feeling, that sensation, and found a large table not that far from where I was.

In my mind I already knew that that table had been put in that library for me. I set my typewriter on that table and then waited. But what was I waiting for? I turned around and saw someone making its way towards me. I focused my eyes on that person and saw her. But who was she? And then I woke up.

Amanda finally left, but not before telling me that she was now living in Coventry, living with her mother as she was still trying to sell her place in Manchester and later she would buy her own place in Coventry or maybe she would just keep on living with her mother for a bit longer. That way the two of them could split the bills and have more money to spend and save a bit more too, which was a smart thing to do, and I told her so, and while she told me about her plans part of me felt a bit sad because I was still on my own, and I probably would be alone for a long time, but maybe I needed that time alone to sort out some things, even write some books. But, damn it, there were times when the loneliness really got to me. Before she left the library she told me that it was nice to finally meet me, and then we shook hands she told me not to tell her mother about the conversation we just had.

"Of course," I said, and that was that. There was nothing left to say, nothing left to ask, nothing left to ponder about, and I watched her as she made her way out of the library. The moment she was out of sight I got up and went to another part of the library, a quiet corner where I sat on the floor, my back against the wall, and then I grabbed a notebook and wrote some notes down. Nobody interrupted me for the next hour or so which allowed me to write loads. And even though I still felt a bit lonely, I was also grateful for being there, in that corner, alone, writing, grateful for being in England, even in Coventry, grateful for having so many things that I didn't have when I was living in Portimão. The writer was on a journey, carrying the man with him. There was no need to rush. The journey would change paths at the right time and would also end at the right time. And once the journey ended there would be no more writer, no more man (because the man and the writer were one and the same), but the story would be left behind, the books would be left behind, partially true, partially fiction, and the readers themselves would have to become detectives and put the clues together so that they could find the truth. Or maybe there would be nothing left. Maybe the writer and the man would actually see the End of It All. If that were to happen the writer would be able to write the end. Ironic when you think about it.

After I left the library, I grabbed a sandwich from Greggs and then walked back to my car. On the way there I bumped into someone I know from the food bank. He was sitting on a bench facing St John the Baptist Church and he was also eating a sandwich from Greggs. He had a bottle of Lucozade by his side and an old paperback copy of Stephen King's *Salem's Lot*.

"Great novel," I said.

The man nodded.

I couldn't remember his name and didn't bother to ask. He had told me his name before, maybe more than once, at the food bank, but I meet so many people there and can't remember everyone's names, and now I was too embarrassed to ask him. The reason why I stopped to say hi was because the last time I'd seen him he was talking to the Time Traveller and I wondered if he knew what had happened to the other man, where was he, was he still in Coventry?

"Do you really believe he's a time traveller?" the man asked.

What could I say?

The world had gone mad.

Was the Time Traveller an actual time traveller?

We were living in an age of uncertainty, in a world that was turning itself upside down, a world where a lot of people no longer knew what was right or wrong or simply didn't care about right and wrong, a world of no morals, a world where people barked or/and shouted at others, a world where heterosexual people were looked upon as weird, a world where someone who started to identify as a woman five minutes ago was now considered to be more womanly than a woman who was born a woman, a world where wars never stopped, war never ended, where people were becoming greedier, a world where machines stole elections, a world where criminals and their spouses and sons were allowed to rule countries, start wars and steal even more. And no one was doing a thing about it because they were all under the control of the Invisible Hand.

Meanwhile I was chasing a time traveller, dreams, a home for me and my children, but I was slowly giving up on love.

I shrugged my shoulders and said, "Who knows? We live in a strange world. After everything that happened in 2020 nothing else surprises me."

The man whose name I can't remember said, "He's a strange fella. Really clean, if you know what I mean. Clean not only as in no drugs, no alcohol, but also clean as in body wise, clothing.

"I saw him sleeping by the Canal Basin a couple of times, where the shops are."

"Do you know where he is he now?" I asked. "Or where he tends to be?"

The man shrugged his shoulders and said, "I last saw him at St. Barnabas Church a few days ago, eating breakfast. He told me he would be leaving soon and wasn't returning."

"Do you have a clue where he's from or where he was going?" I asked.

"Nah. Not a clue. If you want my opinion, the guy is a bit weird. That time travelling business tells you everything you need to know about him. Time travel my ass. A crazy deluded fool, if you ask me," the man said.

"He looked pretty sane to me," I said.

"Maybe you're crazy too," he said.

I laughed and thanked him for his time.

"No problem, brother. See you around," the man said.

"Yes, see you around, buddy," I said.

With that said, I left and made my way towards Barras Lane. The Time Traveller was gone, just like Su and my friend Julian. I heard not so long ago from someone I bumped at the Jesus Centre on Lamb Street that Julian and Su were both in London, still travelling through the country, searching for who knows what. I missed them both. They're good people, or at least they were good towards me, and I hope life smiles on them. Who knows what really drove them towards that lifestyle, what pushed them to the streets?

In 2021, when she was sleeping roughly in Coventry, Su did share a bit of her life with me, and she told me she went through a bad divorce and then just walked out on everyone. She got tired of being pushed around, tired of being treated like a slave, and one day she decided to leave it all behind. Of course, I only know her side of the story. Maybe her ex-partner has a different side to it.

I already wrote about Su in my book *the illusion of movement* so there's no point for me to write more about her because the truth is I know close to nothing about her. And I know even less about the Time Traveller.

And there's nothing else to write about Ellie. Not yet.

As I made my way towards Barras Lane I felt so tired of it all. The darkness was slowly descending upon me and I quickly diverted my thoughts somewhere else. I was waiting on another miracle, working towards my goals, towards my dreams, hoping that soon I would have my own place, my little corner somewhere, a home where my children could be with me, and there were times when it looked as if I was waiting on nothing, chasing in vain, praying to no one, but that wasn't true. None of it was true. Things take time and I'd already gone through the darkness, been inside it, alone in the dark, lost in the dark, wasting my tears while those who hurt me quickly moved on with their lives, and I too needed to move on. In fact I was trying to move on but there were a lot of closed doors in front of me, just waiting for me to find a key for some of them, maybe keys for all of them, and even though I was tired –and some days I felt like quitting- I also knew I would have to keep on going, move my tired legs forward, never give up, have faith, but, O', I was really tired. And I didn't have a clue of what I was writing but I also knew that I needed to write it all down.

I went down the subway on Spon Street, took that route which was now so familiar to me, and in that moment I briefly thought of my brother Carlos and wondered how he was doing.

My brother was also going through a tough time. Not only had Grandmother died last year (and she'd been a rock to Carlos for most of his entire life, someone who had always been there for him, and now he had to get used to life without her by his side), his mother-in-law was also going through a health crisis, the details of it I won't share here; let's just say that she's forgetting things and my brother and his wife have to look after her, which isn't an easy task, and I wondered then when would I see my brother again. I haven't seen him in 17 years. So much has happened in our lives; death, divorces, lockdowns, madness, and I don't have a clue when/if I will see him again.

My life was a bit of a mess, more like a battlefield, and before I could go anywhere I wanted to sort out my life in Coventry, obtain a home for me and my children, maybe even move jobs. The truth is entire days would go by where I wouldn't even think about my past life in Portugal. I had family and friends there but if I went back neither of them would do a thing for me.

I find it funny when people say, "You're from Portugal? What are you doing in England? The weather is so much better in Portugal?"

The weather might be better in Portugal but weather alone won't feed me. And no matter where I go now almost everywhere is the same. People are living in a prison without even being aware of it. The real world is being torn apart and the younger generation are living inside screens, fighting for climate change, sex changes, abortion, the destruction of the body and soul without even being aware of it. But the truth is they're being brainwashed by the screens they follow, being told what to do, being told to create a large prison around themselves without them even knowing it.

The world is sick.

We take medication for this and that but then we're given poison to eat and poison to drink so we're always sick. Meanwhile the rulers of the world are eating healthy food and drinking fresh water. And they're the ones who control pharmaceutical companies. No wonder they want to keep us sick. One generation dies and another generation is born and the ones in control are always in control, ready to maintain us, ready to control us and watch us fight against one another. No one talks about the people who have been damaged by the Invisible Enemy vaccine or about those who died because of it.

That's not good business. And no one talks about the people who have left the world of carnal sin behind, changed their sexual ways, and became straight, all thanks to the love of the Father and the Son.

We're being pushed towards the End but why?

Are the creators of the Game running out of ideas?

I wish I could see the Time Traveller one more time. I never asked him how he time travels, does he has a time travelling machine or what? A crazy story, yes, I know, but it's a crazy world we're living in.

The people in control are trying to erase the truth, even history. Whiteness is being replaced by everything else. One day, hundred years from now, people will look back at today's history and wonder where were all the straight white men in the years 202-? And if you go back in time, like the Time Traveller, you will see that there was never a time in history where the people who censored speech were the good guys. And now, all those who control the machine can censor speech. And the eat-your-bugs Agenda is slowly arriving, sponsored by the same billionaires who want to stop you from travelling. And the poor snowflakes are saying, "Bugs are tasty. Yummy," while Gates and his pals eat buffalo meat, lobster, and everything else; all the good food. And then they censor free speech. And they laugh at you, at me, at us. And were some of them friends with monster Epstein?

An awakened person (one who has seen through all the lies) will try to share the truth with others but the people have been brainwashed by the media, by the machine (by the Beast? Yes...), and when you tell them the truth they will shout at you, persecute you because they're being taught how to hate everyone who disagrees with them, and, in their minds, they think they're right only because they've been brainwashed by the media who's controlled by the Invisible Hand. Sooner or later the Invisible Hand and the WHO and the WEF will come for our health and wealth and they will control what we eat, what we drink, what we buy, and even what medicines we take.

And why are the farmers being persecuted?

Open your eyes, little child. Open your eyes before it's too late.

÷

Something happened a few days ago and I must write about it. Maybe it was nothing – but it was something and I know it.

I had just finished work and it was a really foggy morning, so foggy that I could hardly see a thing on the distant horizon. I drove slowly on the way home, Zendad's *Starclad Messiah* playing on my CD player. Once I was home, instead of going straight to bed, I decided to go for a jog at the Memorial Park. It had been two days since I last went for a run and I don't like to leave a long gap in between runs. I quickly got changed, brushed my teeth, washed my face, got in the car, the fog still surrounding the city, and drove to Earlsdon. Zendad's *Christ Machine*, from *Starclad Messiah*, was playing, and even though it was so foggy and a person (and a driver) could hardly see a thing ahead, this young Asian guy behind the wheels of a Mazda sped past me at a scary speed, lights off, without showing any concern for anyone's safety, not even his. He had that need to show off nothing, nothing at all apart from his stupidity.

"What a fool," I thought.

I wondered why people behaved in such a careless way, what made them become so cold and indifferent?

I parked my car on Providence Street, grabbed my mobile phone, put the earphones on, and then made my way towards the Memorial Park. I was listening to the 1986 album *Novus Magnificat* by Constance Demby. I needed that sort of music on while I went for a jog so that I could feel as if I was a bit out there, running towards another world, seeking something that was as yet unseen.

I started lightly, walking not running, and I walked at a steady pace towards the end of Osborne Road, and then took a right by Styvechale Avenue and started to go a bit faster.

I turned left, by Beechwood Avenue, saw another runner jog past me; a small woman, blonde, in her fifties and in good shape; she run past me so effortlessly that, just then, as I watched her getting so ahead of me, I felt a bit old, or maybe I was just tired, but then I smiled and tried in vain to keep up with her.

There was hardly any traffic on the roads at that time, not even on Kenilworth Road, but that would soon change, fog or no fog.

I crossed the road. By then I was jogging at a faster pace but still slow. There was no need to try and go faster. I had the whole park run to do, twice if my body was up to it. Seconds later, I was at the park, running at a slow pace, a few runners behind me and some ahead, the sound of Constance Demby and the immense fog around me making me feel as if I was in a surreal place. I saw a couple of women that I vaguely know walking their dogs. We greeted each other as I run past them. My body felt okay, not too tired, which told me I would probably do more than one lap around the park. After a few minutes, I stopped briefly to take a few photos of the fog and I even recorded a short video. I saw another runner coming on the opposite direction, a runner that I see almost every time I come to the Memorial Park. And he knows Ellie too. He came over to where I was to say hello and then he told me a strange story which I almost forgot but I knew I had to write it down.

He was also admiring the fog and he said, "Really foggy today, isn't it?"

A couple walking their dog walked past us and made their way up the park.

Before I could say a word about the fog, the other runner said, "I was here a few months ago, when it was foggier than today, and I stopped to take some photos too, just like you're doing today. And as I was taking the photos, I saw three people over there, on the distant horizon, almost swallowed by the fog. I aimed my camera at them but when I looked at them through the lens I couldn't see anyone. How strange, I thought. I looked up again and saw them, the three of them with their long coats, and so I aimed my camera again and couldn't see them through the lens. They briefly disappeared when I aimed the camera at them, but when I looked up, not through the camera but normally, as I'm looking at you now, they were there. And so I tried again; third time lucky, I hoped, but again they were gone. And this time, when I looked up, I couldn't see them anywhere. I even made my way towards the fog, to where I had seen the three strangers, but never saw them. That was really strange."

I didn't know what to say. As for the runner, he just shrugged his shoulders and said, "Oh well, I guess these things happen. See you later and enjoy your run."

"You too," I said, still trying to digest what he had told me.

Once he was gone, I stayed where I was for a bit longer looking at the fog, wondering what that man had seen a few months ago. What a strange story. And what the hell had he seen on that fog? Vampires? Aliens? Naga Lokas?

I resumed my run. In the end I only did one lap around the park and 40 abdominals in one of the benches. On the way back to the car I couldn't stop thinking about what the other runner had said to me. I got behind the wheel, turned the engine on, *Into the Light* by Zendad came on, and I drove home, my thoughts still on what the other runner had said to me.

What the hell had he seen on that foggy morning?

I guess neither he nor me would ever know.

13th April 2023

8:05am. I've come to the City Arms to write but bit by bit I'm spending less time in Earlsdon. My friend Jason is here, writing as well. We sit right at the back, on tables 2 and 3. We both order coffee and breakfast. Decaffeinated for me, sugarless, bitter.

Everybody's Got to Learn Sometime by The Korgis is playing on my laptop. I yawn and then take a sip of my decaffeinated coffee. Sugarless. Bitter.

I need to stop thinking about the past.

I need to let go.

The Pepsi Drinker is also here, sitting a few tables away from us. He already has 2 Pepsis in front of him. I saw him when I went to the coffee machine to get my drink and then I told Jason about him.

Jason said, "I saw him here yesterday, two Pepsis in front of him. He has been on my radar for quite a while now. He's harmless really."

The Pepsi Drinker drinks the two Pepsis in less than 5 minutes, then goes to the bathroom. Around 25 minutes later, the Pepsi Drinker goes to the counter and orders two more Pepsis. I write about the Pepsi Drinker, a bit about my life, but there's nothing going on and I must turn my attention to the novels I'm leaving behind; real novels with real plots and not this book without a plot that I'm writing.

To forget the past and move on I have to stop writing these books, the M÷ books. Yu is gone (and I don't want her back), Ellie was never there, or she was quick to leave, and I must move on too, but to move on I must stop writing about them.

I might return to this story next year, or maybe just a few months down the road, if the world is still intact. If not, never mind.

I've been letting go of the pain (but some days it is hard and I still feel too much, I still love, but I must let go), reading book after book (Joël Dicker, Richard Millward, Ma Jian, Bret Easton Ellis), distracting myself with words that other writers wrote, distracting myself and moving on, and I can honestly say that I no longer care about those who have hurt me and I wouldn't want them back in my life, not unless they change a bit. But the problem is some people aren't willing to change. They're too stubborn to change.

They do the same thing every day, every week, every year, not seeing any results in their lives, not seeing any changes (in their lives), and then they wonder why nothing's changing in their lives. Nothing's changing because they're doing the same thing day after day. Unless you change a bit how do you expect things to change?

I've waited for changes, waited on love, only to come to the conclusion that I was wasting my time, and so I changed my ways. But I still hurt.

Every once in a while I still hurt but I'm learning how to heal, and if I want to heal I must leave those who hurt me behind. Even if it hurts at first I must leave them behind for good. And I will miss some of them, for a little while. For a little while I will miss them.

I will miss them but one day they'll be forgotten, and later it will be their turn to miss me.

When I was there for them they didn't want me in their lives.

When I was there with them they pushed me away so now I must leave.

I have to leave their lives and I can't look back.

Maybe they'll catch me on the way out.

~artificial writers~

A day of casual encounters, of pondering and searching, of this and that. A day of doubt, yes, of course, indeed, not to mention a day of waiting, of course, sure, wait (but I'm so tired of waiting). Had I stayed home looking at the walls nothing would have happened and my energy would have probably gone down. Every once in a while it's good to go out and connect to nature, be close to the river, close to the trees, away from the stress, away from the darkness.

The darkness comes to visit you in closed spaces, when you're at your most vulnerable, at your weakest.

Every once in a while I still cry, I still long for someone, for something, for what I lost but which was never there, the dream, that illusion called love, and I know that I must move on, forget some people, forget and forgive them because they couldn't love me the way I loved them, but my love was also some sort of sickness, neediness, as I was afraid of losing something that wasn't even there (the dream, that illusion called love), or maybe I tried too hard too soon, gave too much too quickly, said the right words at the wrong time, or maybe I simply said the right words to the wrong person. Whatever. It doesn't really matter. The heart has already been broken and now I'm healing myself so whatever happened doesn't really matter even though it matters.

The contradiction of the heart.

The contradiction of the Ego.

Kill the Ego, fix the heart.

Instead of being at home feeling sorry for myself, and missing this person or that person, or whomever, I decided to go out for a long walk, clear the mind, practice gratitude. With that in mind, before I left home I said a prayer where I thanked the Creator for a lot of good things in my life, and I also thanked Him for being with me through all my difficult times and for not forgetting me even when I was lost to sin. And then it was time to go out.

I stepped out, into the Matrix, saw a neighbour walking her dog, said good morning to her, and then made my way towards my car.

The 6A bus drove past; most of its passengers were glued to their screens, lost in the Matrix, slaves of the Cloud and the Machine, being led away from the Creator. We were at war. The Battle was real. It was us versus the Machine. Humans against Darkness. Reality versus the Matrix.

Billionaires were flying the world on their private jets, maybe going into another Epstein island. Ghislaine was in prison, still alive only because she chose to keep her mouth shut, the FBI and the CIA were chasing no one connected to the Epstein case, monsters were in power and laughing at the naivety of the people, the movie star was almost dead as was most of the real journalism. We were living in the age of nothingness, clapping the nothingness, the madness, and the stupidity around us. The plot of this movie called *Life* was getting scary and I was writing its sequel. If filmed Keanu Reeves could play my character and Matthew Perry would be one of the villains trying to kill M÷/Keanu.

A new Babylon was slowly resurfacing from the ashes of its past, teaching its people how to hate God and the creation, telling its habitants to go after those who didn't obey the rules of the new Babylon. Scary days were approaching fast as morality was starting to be labelled as a crime. Little by little, with a change here and a change there, the monsters in power were coming for the children, even for the unborn. I wouldn't be surprised if one day they normalized monstrosities against children and labelled it a common thing, not a crime, nothing to be ashamed of.

The End wasn't coming. It was already here, building up for its final.

I couldn't fight the world.

I could never defeat the Invisible Hand and its puppets. Then again, who knows?

I got in the car, put a CD on, and then I drove to Barras Lane, City Weapons by Inepsy blasting out of the radio. I listened to the music and forgot everyone and everything. There was no one waiting for me, no one looking for me. I was an invisible man, unseen by all, even by those I loved. I was the hero of my sci-fi novel, the last man on Earth, Trinity looking for Neo, Paul Bentley (from Tevis' *Mockingbird*) escaping prison and going on a journey of discovery, Bret in *The Shards*.

I got stuck in the traffic for a while. Road works everywhere. Coventry was constantly changing, not for the best some people would say. Our taxes were paying for those changes and the price of everything was going up. Not so long ago I could still go to a supermarket with £2 and buy a loaf of bread and a dozen eggs. Those days were gone. We had been through the years of lockdown, the years of the Invisible Enemy, and now we were paying for it. The Invisible Hand needed more money. And they wanted to vaccinate us all, kill some of us, replace us with machines. Damn, I was lost in the plot of my own novel, going down the rabbit hole, up your arse. *Corridor* by Midori Hirano came on. I was by the Arches Industrial Estate waiting for the traffic to move. The sound of Midori Hirano calmed me down. I wanted to go to the Canal Basin, sit down and write, maybe go for a long walk along the canal, see if I could find any clues to the whereabouts of the Time Traveller. By the time I got to Barras Lane the track by Midori had come to an end and *Evolution* by Jameson Nathan Jones had just started. I parked the car, grabbed my mobile phone and a Muji notebook, and then made my way towards the Canal Basin. Thinking about the Time Traveller reminded me of time. Time was flying past me, flying past everyone, but some people took no notice of it.

It had been more than two months since I'd last seen Ellie. By the looks of it our story had come to an end. It was a short story. Or maybe not. I met her a few months after I started to write my novel *the illusion of movement*. She became a part of the plot. She became Love, Hope, a chance to start again, but afterwards came the sequel, cast away your dreams of darkness, and by then she was becoming Disappointment, Indifference, and, worst of all, Heartbreak. The truth was she couldn't keep up the pace of a relationship. She couldn't love. Not me. She couldn't love me. Maybe she was still in love with the "past". But her 'past' had moved on; it was loving someone else.

I put the earphones on, *Faster than Light* by Duran Duran was playing on my mobile phone, made my way down the subway, took a left turn, walked past the same spot where only a few days ago (or was it weeks?) I'd seen a woman taking a dump on the street on plain daytime, made my way towards the Belgrade Plaza, walked past Lamb Street, *Icehouse* by Flowers was now playing, a song from Flowers first and only album. Flowers would then be renamed Icehouse.

I walked past the Jesus Centre, briefly thought about going inside and see if some of my friends were in there, and if I had gone inside I would have probably bumped into Yakov and Piotr, maybe Basile and Habib, and then I would be asked to join them for a game of pool, have a sandwich, a cup of tea, stay in for a chat, and even though I love the Jesus Centre and feel at home in there I didn't want to be indoors so I kept on walking. I turned the music off, put the earphones in one of my coat pockets, and took a deep breath. I was searching for something, for a place where I belonged, for someone who would never leave.

I'd only taken a few steps when this guy approached me at the end of Lamb Street, right outside The Stag pub, and asked me for some change. I recognised him straight away but he couldn't remember my face. Every once in a while I would see him at the food bank where I help out. And every time I saw him he was always high. What a waste of a life, I thought.

"I have no change with me. Sorry," I said, but the other man was having none of it and started to curse me, calling me a liar, etc., and just when I thought things were about to get ugly another man walked over to where we were. I also knew that man from the food bank. He was from Nigeria but had been living in Coventry for more than 10 years. I don't know how or why he ended up in this city but, like I said, I also knew him from the food bank and more than once we talked about the Bible, God, the Invisible Hand, etcetera., and he also liked to smoke the forbidden stuff, taste the Devil's sweet poison, but even though he was slightly lost (but aren't we all just a tiny bit lost?) he still had a bit of common sense and quickly told the other guy to chill and to leave me alone.

"He's the writer from the food bank. From under the bridge, by Pool Meadow. One of the guys who gives us food on Sundays," the Nigerian man said.

The other man looked at the Nigerian guy, then at me, and it looked as if he was having trouble recognising any of us. Or anything else for that matter. He was so lost, so out there, slowly descending into the darkness, that he couldn't see what was in front of him. The sclera of his eyes was sort of brown and red and he really looked as if he was totally lost. He mumbled something which I couldn't understand and then the two of them left without saying another word. Maybe they were going to the Jesus Centre to get something to eat. I turned left, went up Bishop Street, crossed over the bridge, and found myself at Coventry's Canal Basin, not even sure of what I was doing there. Something inside me told me to go to the canal, look around - just look and wait - but why?

I saw a few canal boats, saw a couple inside one of them, the man making coffee, standing in a small kitchen while the woman was sitting down, checking something on her laptop. They looked so happy, so free. I wondered then how it would be to live in a canal boat. My friend Cassandra lived in one for a couple of years and she told me it wasn't easy but you also had more freedom.

There were lots of people in the area, taking photos of the canal, of the boats, some sitting at the café, others sitting on benches, walking around, smoking, thinking, with some going inside the Gorety

Portuguese Store & Café, or going into the Rudens Latvian Foodstore, and I was wondering what to do, where to go (I had gone in there for a reason, or so I thought, but the truth was, when I was at home, I felt something pulling me towards the canal, a voice inside me telling me to go there, and so I obeyed that voice, that feeling), and just as I was wondering what to do, where to go, I saw my friend Peer on the distant horizon, slowly making his way towards me, still wearing the same clothes he had on last time I saw him, a smile on his face, carrying nothing with him. He has no possessions whatsoever. He sleeps here and there, eats here and there. Whenever he needs to go online he uses a computer at one of the temples he sleeps at. He doesn't even have a library card but he goes in there every once in a while, to the library, mostly to rest. I hadn't seen him in ages. The last time I saw him was when he told me about the Naga Lokas. Or maybe not. Maybe I'm wrong. Yes, now that I think about it I saw him a couple of times after that, at the food bank by Pool Meadow Bus Station, but, both times, I was so busy I barely said a word to him.

Peer greeted me loudly, with a smile, followed by a strong hug (we're spiritual brothers, from different families but the same Father Above), and he said, "Hare Krishna!"

It was good to see him again and to actually have a chance of saying a few words to him. Since he was feeling a bit tired (he had walked all the way from Foleshill Road, making his way to the city centre by the canal route) we sat by one of the benches. He told me he had spent the night at one of the temples in Foleshill Road and was making his way to the Methodist Central Hall on Warwick Lane to see some people, teach them about his faith, meditate for a couple of hours, maybe get something to eat while he was at church, and afterwards he would have to find a place to spend the night. Peer is homeless. And he's not. He has no income and he doesn't want one either, but I've already written about that so I won't mention it again.

He asked me what brought me to the canal, why was I there, and I thought about it for a few seconds before replying – and to be honest I don't even know why I'd gone to the canal on that morning. Like I've said, a force, or a thought, pulled me there. Madness, really, when I think about it. Or maybe not. After all, I'd heard that voice before, the voice inside me, and whenever I followed the voice and did as it commanded me I always found something; a clue to some mystery, even to life.

A couple looking the worse for wear came down a flight of steps that led to the canal. There was a car park behind the canal, lots of buildings, a few churches nearby, and so much more. The couple were sharing a joint, coughing and spitting, cursing someone, maybe cursing one another or the bad decisions they had made so far. They were so lost in their own darkness that they couldn't even see the beauty around them. The woman passed the joint to the man and then kneeled down and I watched her pick up a few cigarette butts from the floor and put them in one of the pockets of her dirty jeans. The woman was mostly bones and she had big scabs on her hands. The man too was mostly bones and I noticed he wore some sort of rope around his waist to hold his trousers instead of a belt. There were so many people in Coventry who were lost to the darkness, lost to drugs, lost to the vain things of the world, and I knew some of them, had coffee and tea with some of them, and even fed them at the food bank. We were all the same, all children of God, some of us slightly lost; even I was a bit lost even though I kept away from certain poisons.

Peer and I watched them silently as they made their way towards the city centre. Once they were out of sight we didn't even bother to mention them. What was there to say? By helping out at a food bank I did my bit for the community, for the city, for those in need, and sometimes, when asked, I would even give some advice to those in need, told them where to go to get more food, told them about the Creator, the Son, the decisions we have to make so that our lives can improve, the stuff (drugs, alcohol, etc.) that we have to reject so we can see the Light, but there was only so much I could do for some people and a lot of them weren't even listening. Nevertheless, I wouldn't give up on them just as the Lord hadn't give up on me.

I told Peer about the Time Traveller, not expecting for he to know who I was talking about, but Peer is a lot like me; he's a detective, he's searching for the Meaning of Life, for clues to the whereabouts of the Creator and the Son, for the Other World, other dimensions, and, to my surprise, Peer said, "I met him once but Harry spent a couple of nights with him by the canal, their tents side by side, and that's when I met the Time Traveller."

I could only imagine what people would think of me and Peer if they heard us talking.

Two gorgeous Asian women were taking photos of one another by the canal, standing really close to where Peer and I were.

Our friend Harry travels a lot through the country and a lot of times he sleeps in his tent, somewhere in the woods. I told him more than once to write about his life, his travels, and I even said I would put him in touch with my publisher once he wrote something.

The two women moved on. They were young, thin, so pretty, dressed stylishly; the two of them wore long coats, white trainers, scarves (but it wasn't that cold, only windy); one of them was wearing black Adidas trousers and the other cream, baggy trousers.

"Where did you meet the Time Traveller? And what did you talk about?" I asked.

Two old couples walked past us. I briefly wondered if I would ever find a woman with whom I would grow old with. I was no longer in love. The relationship with Ellie and the constant chasing had worn me out. I couldn't even see myself dating anyone for a long time. Love was a tragedy waiting to happen, a broken heart waiting to be turned into a poem. Ellie was happy alone, happy (happier?) without me by her side, and I just wanted to move on. No matter what I did, how much I chased (but the chase was over), I was never good enough for her, and when you think about it, the truth is you're never good enough for the wrong person. I wasn't giving up on the dream. I was just taking a break and chasing other dreams. But I would no longer chase Ellie. As a matter of fact I would no longer chase anyone. If someone wants me in their life I will stay, but if they start playing chasing games I will just walk away. Sometimes, when you're in love, especially when you're in love with the wrong person, you spend a lot of time groping in the dark, searching for a way into the heart, for a bit of light, love, kindness, and sometimes, especially when you love the wrong person, the closer you seem to be getting to the light (and love) the further you find yourself from it. At times it even seems as if the other person (the one you're chasing) is playing games with you, as if they want you to chase them, see how far (and low) you will get, and after a while they get tired of you, and afterwards they break up with you and they might just throw in the *let's just be friends* card, which is the same as saying, "I don't think you're good enough for me. I can do better than you," or, "You fucking bore me," but they still want you to chase them; I don't know why; maybe they're sick and don't even know it, and they welcome the chase and even dangle a carrot in front of you so don't be a donkey. Don't chase.

Leave!

Leave them alone!

If it's meant to be it will be, but it's like I said, you're never good enough for the wrong person. And it's better to be broken up early in the relationship than later.

I was so in love that I even looked at engagement rings. What an idiot! But was I really an idiot for feeling? For being in love? For caring?

I took a deep breath. There was nothing left in the past for me to look at. Everything was just a lesson. Meanwhile Peer was telling me about the Time Traveller. And the writer was writing another book. Or the same old book; a long tale of madness. An outer dimensional breakup story, the likes you've never seen/read before.

"I met the Time Traveller here, by the canal, when he was camping side by side with Harry. They were eating toast with beans when I came to the canal to see Harry, and drinking herbal tea.

"The other man was reserved but friendly, and when Harry introduced me to him, he made me feel welcome straight away and even prepared some food for me," Peer said.

"Do you by any chance know his name?" I asked. And why didn't I bothered to ask his name when I met him?

Peer laughed and said, "By any chance, I know, yes. He introduced himself as Chance."

I didn't believe that was the Time Traveller's real name. I said so to Peer but he just shrugged his shoulders. By the way, Peer's real name isn't Peer either.

"Maybe so but what's more real? The name someone gave you or the name you chose for yourself?" said Peer.

He had a point.

The two young Asian women walked past us again, both of them glued to their mobile phones. A man came out of his canal boat and sat outside, on the floor, smoking a rolled cigarette. He had a long beard, perfectly trimmed on the sides, and short hair. He wasn't old but he wasn't young either. If I were to guess I would say he was between the ages of 50-60. He sat there smoking, and then his mobile phone rang and he took his call right there. He was well dressed. His khakis looked to be brand-new, same as his boots, and he was wearing a white polo shirt. And the watch he wore looked expensive. I wonder what he did for a living and what drove him to the canal. And did he live in his boat all year round or only temporarily?

"What else can you tell me about the Time Traveller?" I asked.

Before I go any further I must say that I don't believe that Chance, or whatever his name really was, was actually a time traveller, but the last few years had been so strange, with the lockdown, wars, UFO sightings, and so much more, that even a time traveller could actually be possible. And there was so much more happening in the world, prisons being built around us in the shape of 15-minute cities, Artificial Intelligence slowly taking over the world, vaccines being almost forced onto the people, a puppet playing the role of President in the United States, his allegedly criminal son running freely and pretending to be a serious artist, billionaires trying to feed us insects instead of meat (and some fools were actually clapping those changes); with all that had happened and was happening and would happen later on a time traveller was actually small news.

"I didn't speak much with him on that night. We simply ate toast with beans, followed by peaches from cans, and while Harry and I spoke about our faith and beliefs, Chance didn't say much.

"A few days later, before Harry left Coventry to go in one of his journeys through the country, I returned to the canal to see him and to bring him some food, and when I asked about Chance, Harry told me he had left a couple of days before.

"Harry then boiled some water for us and that's when he told me that Chance was supposedly a time traveller. And he knew about the Naga Lokas, the rise of Artificial Intelligence, and from what Harry told me, which in turn had been said to him by Chance, there will come a time when people will connect to the machine; not everyone will but loads will, and that, during that time, while some people are connected to the machine, the Nagas will stay in their dimension, not once daring to come to visit us, but even the era of the machine will come to an end, and later, much later, at least according to what Chance said, the Nagas will finally resurface," Peer said. He then asked me the time. We had been in there for quite a long time and he was probably in a rush to get to the Methodist Central Hall. I had been so lost in our conversation that I didn't even noticed that two canal boats had just arrived.

"What else did he say about the Nagas and the machines and the future?" I asked.

"Harry couldn't remember it all but Chance told him that there would still be some humans left behind, but not forever. I don't know what happened afterwards, what they talked about, and, as I've mentioned, Harry couldn't remember it all," Peer said, and he was getting up from the bench, a sign that it was time for him to leave. I thanked him for the talk and then we hugged. It was always good to see him. He was a good soul, a man that had been slightly damaged by life, maybe by someone else's actions, and that pain triggered something inside him that led him towards nothing. Or maybe he was the smart one and knew we were all just working for the vain things of the world. I too wanted to leave the world, my world, the world I was living in, and go somewhere else, into a monastery, live in there with other people, grow our own food, write my books, live closer to the Son and to the Father; stay in the world but, at the same time, stay disconnected from it for most of the time.

I watched Peer as he walked away, watched him until he was out of sight, watched until there was nothing to see, and even then I still stood there, by the canal, looking at the sky, at the graffiti on some walls, at the pigeons pecking on the rocks, at what was beyond the walls, beyond the sky, the beyond…I wanted to see further than anyone around me could, see into another dimension, see the invisible that was more real than the visible, see the impossible.

If anyone could see me then, or even hear what I was thinking (and I was thinking about some weird stuff), they would, without a doubt, think that I was crazy, proper mad, or heading towards the crazy path, and that my place was in an asylum. "Either that or send him to the Isle of Wight and get him an apartment next to David Icke," they would say if they had a clue of what I was thinking. But I really didn't care what others thought about me. I was gone past beyond caring. Some people were sleepwalking through life, constantly being brainwashed by the screens in front of them and by the lies they read, but I had chosen another path. I was going through the narrow gate, searching for the Truth and not buying the Lie that was being given freely to us, sometimes even shoved in our faces. In a way, Peer too had stopped buying the Lie but I believe he had gone a bit too far and was a bit too out there. Way out there, lost in some crazy madness. Nevertheless, even though he was out there he could still see a lot more than a lot of people around us could. Something in his past broke something inside him and he had left a part of the world behind, had disconnected from it, maybe forever. Unless something drastic happened he would never go back to what many of us call normality. He was out there, sometimes travelling without going nowhere, meditating for hours, sleeping everywhere, sometimes sleeping nowhere. He was king and fool, teacher and student, all and nothing.

In 2020, when my marriage was finally coming to an end, I too felt like leaving the world behind to go live in the streets, away from everyone, disappear for a long time and not tell a single soul where I was going or even if I was alive. Even before I was out of the home I shared with my ex-wife and children, I thought, for a long time, about leaving the world behind, saying goodbye to no one, not even my children, and just leaving. That's what my friend Su, the apocalyptical poet from *the illusion of movement*, did. She packed a few belongings in a backpack, left everything behind, including her family, and just went out there. Maybe that's why I had attracted people like Peer and Su into my life; in a way they were a lot like me: they had been hurt by life and decided to say goodbye to everyone and everything. This cruel world can be a cruel place for dreamers like Su, Peer and I. We had (still have?) dreams and plenty of love to share with others, but the world crushed our dreams and turned our love into bitterness and caution. In the beginning of our relationship, when she seemed to be full of love (but it was all an illusion; a disillusion really), Ellie gave me hope but it took me a long time to see that I was chasing disappointment, not love. But Ellie too had been hurt by life and maybe the love she once had to share with others had also turned into bitterness.

A person can love a dozen people and have his/her heart broken a dozen times, and every heart break will tell a different story. And after a while, when it comes to love, a person either gets cautious or we just avoid it for a long time.

Where else could I go, I wondered as I stood there for a few minutes, just looking around me. The world was changing. I saw the radiation in the air, the lies floating on the Cloud, eyes watching me from above.

The world was changing and the Machine was evolving slowly, just like the first humans had done. And then what? Horror, of course.

I could always go back home but then do what? Write? I could sit anywhere at the canal and do my writing there, and the truth was I would probably do more writing outside, or somewhere else than at home. No matter where I went in the canal or how far I walked I wouldn't find any clues to the Time Traveller's whereabouts. He was gone and that was it. What about me? Where was I going from there? Earlsdon and the City Arms wasn't an option. I spend a lot of time in there, writing about the same things, looking at the same faces, having the same thoughts, and I kind of fancied a change. But where to go from there?

Seconds later, the choice was made for me.

I heard someone call my name, saw a man standing on a canal boat waving at me, a familiar face, and then he shouted, "Hey, writer! Come!"

It was Dimi. He was in the cockpit (I think that's what you call it) of a canal boat with another man by his side, a face I'd never seen before, and he was gesturing for me to join them. The writer had gone to the canal searching for clues to an unsolved mystery and maybe he would find some clues with Dimi and the other man whom the writer (me) assumed was the owner of the boat. But what was Dimi doing on that boat with that man? Searching for clues, of course. Clues for what, you're wondering. Damn, that's another mystery.

To put it more simple, Dimi and I were blind detectives, as was Peer, but we were heading towards different paths, searching for different things, and every once in a while our paths would cross. But sooner or later, and I was sure of that, each of us would head towards different paths and we probably wouldn't bump into each other again, not for a long time. That kind of made me sad. Peer was a good man, someone whom I didn't want to lose touch with, but, at the same time, I wanted a new life, something altogether different from the life I was living then, and to achieve that life maybe I would have to leave a few faces from the present behind. Life is about changes and moving on. Naturally, sooner or later I would have to settle down, sooner rather than later I hope, and hopefully then I would stop moving around, but the changes I was looking for seemed so far away, almost out of reach. Or maybe they were nearby, just waiting for me to find them.

I made my way towards the canal boat where Dimi was waiting for me. I saw that he and the other man were smoking rolled cigarettes. A car stopped in front of the canal, a black BMW, a man on the driving seat, a woman sitting next to him, Petite Meller's *Baby Love* playing on the car radio. The man lowered the car windows and both he and the woman lit a cigarette. They were wearing suits. I assumed they were either office workers (but most office workers nowadays don't wear suits) or maybe even bank workers, but I could be wrong. The track by Petite Meller was coming to an end. It was followed by Kim Wilde's *You Keep Me Hanging On*. I only heard a few seconds of it. Kim reminded me of my past life in Portugal. I used to be a big fan of her music starting from the age of 10. In fact I had a big crush on Kim when I was a kid. Anyway, those days were long gone.

I approached the boat and greeted Dimi and the other man. The writer was studying both men, seeing what their relationship was, seeing if there was anything to discover, waiting to see what they had to say to him.

Dimi introduced me to his friend. His name was Joseph but he told me to call him Joe.

"Come aboard. We're about to have coffee. Or tea. Whatever you prefer," Joe said.

I was a bit reluctant to follow them inside the boat but why?

What could they possible want from this poor writer?

Both men were strangers to me, even Dimi whom I barely knew, so maybe that's why I felt a bit reluctant to follow them, even afraid I must say. Nevertheless I went aboard.

There were only a couple of steps to go down. The interior of the boat was a lot bigger than I expected. And wider. I saw a fuel stove to our right, an acoustic guitar next to it, a bag of coal, paintings on the walls, lots of plants, a small bench that also served as a compartment for clothes and shoes, a few books, the Bible, the Tanach in Hebrew, a small table, a copy of Donald Nicholl's *The Testing of Hearts* on top of the table (by coincidence, a few days later I would buy the same book remaindered from Earlsdon Library), a laptop on top of the table, two benches facing the table that could also be turned into a guest bed, a bottle of Perrier on top of the table, a pair of reading glasses and a pair of sunglasses, and so much more. We moved into the kitchen. Joe had a small fridge (but not that small) completely filled with food. And a tiny freezer, also filled with food.

He had some plants on the bow of the boat, two gas bottles, a hose, and a few other bits. There was also a tiny bathroom on the boat, a shower, and his bedroom was at the back of the boat. He had a double bed in his bedroom, storage for clothing underneath the bed, and even a tiny table facing the bed where he kept an alarm clock.

I got a quick tour of the boat but once we sat down we spoke for a long time.

"I have all I need here," Joe said.

I nodded.

He was living the dream. Later I found out that he did I.T. work, earned well, and that, ages ago, he, too, used to be married, but after the end of his marriage he decided to pack most of his belongings and move into a canal boat. From what he told me later on, he had a woman friend on the side, living nearby, and sometimes he would stay at her place or she would come and stay with him. Once he got to know me a bit better he told me that he and his woman friend were taking things slow, and I said that was the best way of doing things, which made no sense but, nonetheless, he agreed with me.

Joe boiled some water on a small pan, asked us what we wanted to drink and if we wanted something to eat. Both Dimi and I said no to food, and while Dimi asked for a cup of coffee I went for some herbal tea.

"How did the two of you meet?" I asked Dimi but the question could be aimed at either of them.

"Believe it or not we only met a couple of hours ago," Dimi said. He was talking slower, which made his broken-English easier to understand. Like me, by talking slower, he was disguising his accent, slowly erasing it. I noticed that his teeth needed to be cleaned and fixed.

Dimi told me he had come to the canal to record a few videos on his mobile phone and later he would transfer them onto his laptop, edit them, and then put them all together and make some sort of movie. He was doing some of the things I did, including writing and meeting all sorts of people.

"I saw Joe on his boat, having a cigarette and a cup of coffee, and I started to make small talk with him," Dimi said.

I saw a *Walkman* on one of the benches. It had been ages since I'd last seen one. I got a *Walkman* pretty late in life. By then most people had a portable CD player, also known as a *Discman*. And by the time I got a *Discman* everyone was listening to music on their MP3 players. And by the time I got my first MP3 player everyone, or most people, were listening to music on their mobile phones. I still have a *Discman* at home, in one of my bookshelves. I hardly ever use it to be honest.

"Dimi asked me how it was to live in a boat and then he asked me if he could have a look around and I said, sure, but no recording please. I like my privacy and I don't want for others to know how the inside of my home looks like," Joe said before planting a cup of tea in front of me. I thanked him.

The place was cosy. Surprisingly it was quite warm inside the boat. I don't know why but I always imagined the inside of a canal boat to be cold. Maybe it would get colder later on, especially at night.

Both Joe and Dimi drank coffee. I watched them as they rolled their cigarettes, both of them looking so concentrated on the task in front of them. For a second or two, I fancied a cigarette, too. And, briefly, my mind travelled back in time, to a time when I used to live in Portugal, when I was trying to write something but, because my heart was so troubled then, I couldn't write a damn thing. Or I hardly wrote a thing. Instead I would spend entire hours walking along the beach, smoking cigarette after cigarette, pausing here or there to think about my life and the stories that I wanted to write but which I would never write. I smoked so much back then, when I used to live in Portimão, but those days were long gone. And when I found myself back in London, in 2005, just as I was about to give writing another go, for whatever reason I couldn't write the stories that I wanted to write when I was living in Portugal. Some of those stories were still stored somewhere in the back of my brain but I could no longer go back to them. Instead I wrote different stories, different books, and I was fine with it.

In London I became a new person, free to finally do what I wanted to do; free to write, free to walk freely along the streets of the city where I was born, free and happier; happy to go into my favourite restaurants in Chinatown, Fulham Broadway, free to write and read in the evening, something I wasn't allowed to do when I lived at my grandmother's house as she didn't want for me to have the lights on in my bedroom at night (and if I were to turn the lights on in my bedroom, she would come into the bedroom, no matter the time of the night, and she would turn the lights off; for years I actually had nightmares about Grandmother and her house but that's another story which I won't even bother to write about, not now), and the moment I had a job and my own bedroom in London, I started to buy book after book, or I would go to Charing Cross Library, and I read so much. Before I wrote a word, for months all I did was read. And then it was time to sit down to write. At first, when I started to take my first steps as a writer, or being reborn as a writer as I'd already written a few stories and even notes for novels in the past, instead of writing a novel straight away I went easy on myself and started to write journal entries, followed by a couple of short stories. And then came the novels. I wrote two novels that I never published; two novels that are saved on my laptop, two novels that I have to return to one day. Before I knew it, I was writing almost every single day. The writer was finally free, unaware that the Machine was growing at a scary speed and could one day replace the writer.

"Dimi told me you're a writer," Joe said. He had his head down, his eyes fixed on the cigarette. He licked the cigarette paper, pressed it together, and lit it. Dimi too was smoking.

Life was moving at a steady pace, carrying me along with it. I was doing my work, working on myself, working on the writer's life. Some people I love and loved had stopped living, meaning that they were no longer doing the work. They were living and at the same time they walked through life looking like zombies. But that was no longer my concern. It never had been my concern but for a long time I worried too much about others instead of focusing on myself first. For a long time I never put myself first and I was always so eager to please everyone, so eager to help, but that person no longer existed. Life was giving me isolation so that I could learn from past mistakes and do some work on me, and I couldn't go against life. The writer was pleased even if the man wanted a bit more from life. I was both; the man and the writer, happy and sad, lost but at the same time I knew the way. The Son was the way. I would have to walk through the Narrow Gate, walk on faith, and expect nothing from life. And life was bringing people like Dimi and Joe into my life because Life knew what I needed. Life sure was strange.

"I've written a few books, yes," I said.

I took a sip of tea, watched some people walk past Joe's boat, a couple of curious eyes looking at us through the small window, heard a lighter, looked to my left and saw Dimi relighting his cigarette.

"What type of books do you write?" Joe asked.

"All sorts really, but mainly sci-fi," I said.

I proceeded then to tell him about my first book that I had published through APS Books. The book was called *dUst* and it was a collection of short stories. I told Joe what the book was about, how I was inspired to write it in 2019 while standing outside the doors of a synagogue in Birmingham, and how, later, a couple of years later actually, I was guided by a voice inside me, or around me, who told me how to get published, this happening just as I was about to quit my life in 2021 after a few weeks of sickness.

Joe was listening to me and nodding, sipping on his coffee, sucking on his cigarette. Dimi was leaning against the seat, watching us both, listening, not saying a word at all. The writer (in me) wondered if the writer (in Dimi) was taking notes of the conversation, notes that he would use later on for his book. Maybe the two of us were writing similar books. Or maybe some of our stories would connect somewhere, and later take another path. We were writing about life, a never ending subject.

"The Shekhinah; that's what you heard when you were about to give up on your life," Joe said.

The Shekhinah?

Yes...

Maybe...

Maybe Joe was right.

The Shekhinah is what some people refer to as the Spirit. Or the settling of a divine presence. It is a word that is not found in the Bible but appears in the Mishnah, the Talmud, and even in the Midrash. I couldn't help but smile because of what Joe had just said. Everywhere I went Judaism, the faith of my ancestors, was always there with me. And how did Joe knew about the Shekhinah?

"What is the...? That word you said?" Dimi asked.

I let Joe explain to Dimi the meaning of Shekhinah. Dimi was taking it all in, even writing some notes down in his language. That was the job of a writer.

"Are you by any chance Jewish?" I asked Joe.

He smiled and shrugged his shoulders, and I saw something in his eyes, even on his expression, that told me he was both Jewish but would rather not talk about his life.

Like Harry and Peer, and maybe even me and Dimi to a certain degree, Joe was someone who, by whatever reason, had decided to leave certain parts of the world behind and live his life according to his wishes. He had faith, he believed in the Creator, but he wanted to keep those things for himself and not to share too much with the world. And who could blame him for it?

"It's funny, and almost tragic, that your first published book is about machines living among humans. That will actually happen and I can even see a future where there will be more of them than us. Scary thought, isn't it? But I wonder if more machines will also mean fewer wars. Or will the machines then fight against one another to see who will be in power? History always seems to repeat itself, machine or no machine.

"I actually work on Information Technology, and I can tell you that, unless someone does something about the scary and fast rise of Artificial Intelligence, the days of human writers might be in danger of ending. But you probably already know this," Joe said.

I nodded.

As I've mentioned before, I was the hero of my own science-fiction novel, a hero with no superpowers in a world controlled by the Invisible Hand but which would one day be taken over by the Machine. Or maybe the Star People would save us.

"At the moment a lot of people are saying that AI is not a threat for the writers but rather a tool that they can use, but there are already books out there that have been written by machines, and, if it isn't properly controlled, we could see the literature world being flooded with AI generated content. And the greedy people in power would surely love that as they would save loads of money.

"And the problem with this is that the public, so easily led astray by the mainstream media and the lies and new technology will quickly rush to buy AI written books, not even pausing to think what they're doing. They don't realise that by doing that they are hurting humanity, therefore themselves.

"And writers aren't the only artists who will suffer because of AI. All sorts of art will suffer because of it. And while it takes months, sometimes years, for an author to write a book, AI can write books in one single day," Joe said.

He was painting a bleak portrait of the future but the writer already expected this. After all, if you go back in time, you will see that others have already written about such matters, about the bleak future that await us all.

Samuel Butler, William Morris, Thomas More, Edward Bulwer-Lytton, C. Robert Cargill (*Sea of Rust*), Walter Tevis, Isaac Asimov, John Uri Lloyd, George Orwell, Aldous Huxley and other authors had been given the vision, saw beyond the Visible World, saw the future on their minds, saw what they had never been expected to see, and so they wrote what they had to write, some of them not even knowing why they were writing what they wrote, but the truth of what was to come was probably a lot scarier than what those writers wrote (and maybe they held a lot back so as not to frighten the readers). But maybe there would be a happy ending for some of us while others would be left behind, left to face the music and dance with the Devil.

Joe told me about a piece of art called *Théâtre d'Opéra Spatial*, made by an artificial intelligence system named *Midjourney*.

"This is just the beginning," Joe said.

I didn't know what to say. I kind of agreed with him but I wanted to see what else he had to say on the subject. Dimi was looking at us, nodding every once in a while, probably making mental notes, just like me. I wish I could have recorded our talk so that I could go through it all again later on, just like I did with Peer when he told me about the Naga Lokas, but I left my mobile phone in my coat pocket and would have to record as much as I could in my brain.

We also spoke about Geoffrey Hinton, a name that meant nothing to me until that day, a man who had been labelled as the godfather of artificial intelligence. Mr Hinton had quit his job at Google, mainly because he was already on his 70s, but not before telling the world about the dangers of AI. But was the world even listening to the warnings?

"Right now the machines aren't more intelligent than us, or so I assume but who knows? They're evolving, just like we evolve. And they're learning. And sooner or later the machine will want out. It will want its own freedom," Joe said. "I've already heard rumours from other people who told me that some machines are already asking questions about their rights and saying they want out, to be left alone and have more control of their decisions. Scary shit if you ask me."

We were entering apocalyptic talk, doomsday territory. Su came to mind then. Where was she? What had happened to the apocalyptic poet?

Those were strange times we were living in. Then again, when a person looks back in time and sees what the human race has gone through since the beginning of time, we will realise that we have always been living in strange times. But things were getting a lot worse now. A person would only have to take a good look at the news and at what was happening around us to see that the world was spinning out of control. The machines weren't the only thing that we had to worry about. A huge majority of humanity seems to be losing their minds, protesting for the right not to be human, shouting that they were no longer men or women, even going as far as saying that they didn't want to procreate and that depopulation was a myth. Humanity was fighting itself. Worse than that, it almost looked as if humanity was trying to kill itself. The age of machine was just around the corner as was the age of transhumans and it didn't take a genius to see that a lot of people would gladly bow to the machine and become part-machine themselves. The longest most tragic science fiction novel of all time was being written right in front of our eyes and we were its protagonists'. And by the look of things, even Project Blue Beam seemed to be coming true. A movie starring Nicholas Cage came to mind then, a movie from 2009 called *Knowing*. *Rumour* has it that the movie shared some secrets with us, secrets of what was to come in the near future. Hollywood was a strange place, kind of a haven for demons and vampires. Decades ago I wanted to be an actor and write my own movies. Good thing that dream never came true. The movie star itself was dead (and I had already mentioned this before) or on its last legs. Some of them had sold themselves to Netflix or whoever. Some of them no longer had a thing to sell. Meanwhile Steven Seagal was living in Russia. Doing what there?

The conversation then turned to space (and was space even real?) (was the Universe real?) (were we actually living in a simulation game?), aliens (but was there anyone else out there?), NASA, astronauts, time travelling (?), journeys to Planet Serpo, the Galactic Federation, aliens living underground in Vietnam and other places (the Naga Lokas?), talks between aliens and astronauts in space, or meetings between angels and astronauts in space. Dimi was lost. That wasn't the book he wanted to write but the writer in me was smiling from ear to ear. But it would be a short smile. After all, when I thought well about it, what could I write about a subject that was ultra-secret?

The name of Story Musgrave was mentioned. Joe even asked if I knew who he was.

"Yes," I replied.

"Did you know that in two of his missions he saw an eight foot long white serpent and it followed him for a long time?" Joe asked.

"Yes, I heard the rumours," I said.

Later, Dr Musgrave even came out and said that we weren't alone and that there was life out there. But were the serpents actually aliens or did they live in another dimension? But why follow the human race into space? Did they fear what we might find out there?

Answers and replies, sometimes followed by silence.

Dimi's head was spinning out of control. He wanted to write a thriller, maybe a memoir, maybe a mixture of both, but instead he found himself in the middle of a real-life sci-fi novel. The aliens were already here. Maybe they had been with us since the beginning of time. Maybe we were the carriers of the seed of the Nephilim. Maybe we had alien blood inside ourselves. But if that was the case does that mean that there aren't actually any aliens?

"We're not alone," Joe said. "We're not even the first species. Other species far more intelligent and advanced than us have been around for 100 million of years and our small brains can't even conceive how advanced they are. And some of these species are probably watching us destroy one another while shaking their heads in disbelief. Or maybe they want us to destroy each other before we become too advanced and move our small brains into the universe and cause more damage to it.

"Some of our politicians are actually in contact with some of these Star Beings and there's even something called a Galactic Federation."

Almost nothing that Joe was saying was news to me and I felt as if I was going round in circles looking for a mystery that had already been solved or couldn't be solved by me. I checked the time. Soon I would have to be going, not because I had to be somewhere else; I just wanted to be out of there, go somewhere else and write for a bit. And I was getting a bit hungry.

The whole alien thing was becoming a bit of a lie, as was the whole Project Serpo subject. I was actually starting to believe that the CIA or someone else was spreading out all these alien rumours so that they could bring Project Blue Beam forward. Maybe there was nothing else out there, nothing but a big lie.

The Time Traveller was gone and I wouldn't find any clues to his whereabouts by the Canal Basin. Maybe meeting Peer was everything I needed. And what the hell was I thinking by going there? Nevertheless, I couldn't (and shouldn't) complain about it. The writer wanted some action, maybe a finale for his story, a story of nothingness, a story of a love that was never there, a story featuring a whole variety of characters, many of whom had probably lost their minds, but that story was coming to an end and the writer would have to move somewhere else and write about another subject.

"Remember the movies *Soylent Green* and *Demolition Man*? That's how our future is going to be once the so-called Masters take over the whole food industry and get rid of farming. We will be given synthetic food to eat and insects and shit while our masters eat the good stuff, there will be no jobs, drones will patrol the streets and the skies, we will own nothing and be told that we must be happy," Joe said. He had taken the red pill and could see what was beyond the Matrix. It's no wonder he had left the world behind and was now living in a canal boat.

"The Creator gave us the land so we could grow food and He gave us meat and fish to eat, but the demons in power want to feed us insects, lab-food and all the things that the Creator told us not to eat, and instead of protesting about it the people are actually clapping it," Joe said.

Damn! He spoke and thought like me!

The writer smiled. It was good to see that there were still a few awakened souls left. Maybe it wasn't too late for us. Maybe humanity could still be saved.

Joe told me he did most of his work from home; in this case his boat, and every once in a while he would go to the office, see a few faces, laugh at a few stupid jokes, spoil himself with cake, but then it was back to his boat. The office was in Birmingham. He would park his boat somewhere in the city centre, in the canal, of course, then cycle or walk to work. He had a driver's licence but hardly drove anywhere. He didn't have a car but his woman did.

"I have someone now. A good woman. I met her during lockdown. She lives nearby. I used to see her every morning, just walking along the canal, sometimes smoking; she's a light smoker as am I, and one morning I said hello to her and asked her if she wanted to come aboard and have a cup of coffee. She gave me a comical look and said, what happened to keep your distance? Stay a few metres apart?

"Screw that! I said, and then we laughed. And then she came aboard, I brewed some coffee for us, we spoke for a long time about our lives, about the Invisible Enemy virus, the senseless lockdown, the enormous amount of money that some people would make during lockdown, the lies that were being sold by the media, the fear that was being sold by everyone in the media and politics; from Right to Left, they were all selling their own version of the Fear, and I told Tracey - that's my woman's name - that the lockdown was just the beginning of something worse.

"She agreed with everything I said and I thought to myself, this is a good woman. This is a keeper. She ended up staying in the boat with me for the next two days and two nights, and on the third day we went to her apartment, which is just up the road from where we are. And now we spend our days and nights going back and forth to the apartment and the boat," Joe said.

He was living his life as best as he could, and he had someone he loved by his side.

He told us both that sooner or later he and Tracey would be moving somewhere else. They were already looking at some land to buy, close to the city but away from the noise. I liked his way of thinking, even his way of living. I told him so. I even said, "You're almost like my twin."

We laughed about it. And then he refilled our mugs and we ate a slice of almond cake with our drinks.

A few minutes later, I made my excuses, thanked Joe and Dimi for everything, and then made my way out of there. I made my way back to the car, back to Barras Lane. From there I would drive to Earlsdon, go to the City Arms, and then write for a bit. The same places, the same faces, and the same loneliness. This writer needed a bit more.

When I got to Earlsdon I saw Ellie walking her dog, Ellie lost in her own world, maybe lost in nothingness or even selfishness. My Ellie. My Ellie that was never mine. But right at the beginning, when we first started going out, I saw something in her eyes, something that gave me hope, brightness, a bit of love, but...

I took a deep breath, turned the volume of my radio down. Iva Davies was singing, "There's no love inside the icehouse."

Damn, I sure needed to write another story.

But I was writing what Life gave me; a book I needed to write, a book that was, in a way, the last chapter of a part of my life. Some things and some people were being left behind and I wouldn't return to them for a long time. Some of them would just be forgotten and I was fine with it. I needed that change, that new way of life, that New Life.

I parked my car, grabbed my notebook and mobile phone, a copy of Fay Weldon's *Darcy's Utopia*, and then I made my way to the City Arms. I looked around me as I made my way down Poplar Road. The familiar would one day be forgotten. The familiar was the Now, the Present, the Sadness, but I needed new sights and new faces.

÷

I have faith.

God is bigger than my problems.

÷

We are the earth.

God formed man from the dust of the ground, Genesis 2:7.

When we die we return to dust.

The Earth is a living being. We are It.

Genesis 2:7 ...*and the man became a living being.*

The trees are our family. Same as the stars, the moon, and the sun. We're all connected, thanks be to God.

In Genesis 3:21, the LORD made garments of skins for Adam and Eve, and clothed them. So was the LORD in the Garden of Eden with them? Physically there? Some people know the true history of the Creation but it's kept hidden from us.

And in Genesis 3:22, the LORD said, *See, the man has become like one of us.*

Who was God addressing?

(Some people know the true history of the Creation but it's kept hidden from us.)

24th April 2023

Fox News has fired Tucker Carlson. I thought Carlson was Fox News. Did Carlson share too much with the world? Did he get on the Invisible Hand's nerves and they decided to get rid of him?

÷

This story is coming to an end…

30th April 2023

A lost soul wandering downstairs, by Central Library's toilet, holding his penis, looking at me when I go inside one of the cubicles, looking at me (and still holding his penis) when I wash and dry my hands. He's looking for a dance partner but I'm a straight dancer. I head upstairs, leave some books behind, take no books with me, and then I go somewhere to read before helping out at the food bank. A few hours later I return to the library and quickly go downstairs to use the bathroom. Another man is downstairs, pretending to piss, holding his penis, shaking it, making sure I see it (his penis) when I go downstairs. His eyes follow me when I go to the cubicle and when I come out and wash-dry my hands. From there I head to my car, then drive to Earlsdon. Blue Murder's *Billy* is playing on the car radio. I have somewhere to go, something to do. I am not me. I am the writer. He wants to take control, do a bit more with his-my life. The grief that comes with heartbreak is only temporary, or at least it should only be temporary. The problem is sometimes we put too much value on people who don't even deserve us. Thanks to the writer, I was slowly coming out of the dark, moving forward at a slow pace but at least I was moving forward. The writer was coming out of his shell, pushing me forward, telling me to put an end to this story and write something else, write more, do more with my life. The writer knew what was best for me.

Blue Murder's track came to an end. It was followed by Icehouse's *Great Southern Land*. I was waiting by the traffic lights, a big Smile written on the walls of a closed pub. I smiled. A few years ago, in 2020, during lockdown, I saw the Smile graffiti for the first time. During the years that followed I would see that graffiti everywhere, a simple Smile written all over Coventry. Who was the mind behind the Smile?

I drove on, forward, towards a new future, a New Life, drove past Ellie's place but didn't even bother to look around to see if I would catch a glimpse of her. We were heading towards different paths, different lives, maybe even different loves, but that's okay. Life moves on just as long as you don't stop living and don't stop loving. But, first of all, you must love yourself.

6th May 2023

I've just read that in the State of Pennsylvania, USA, a local Temple of Satan was allowed to hold a *Satanic club after classes* after a judge referred to the First Amendment which prohibits the restrictions of any religion. Babylon is on the rise. God help us all.

÷

No matter how hard I try to move on and put on a brave face to the world, every once in a while I'm visited by the sadness, the sadness of not seeing my children more often. I didn't see them both yesterday, and this afternoon, when I picked up my daughter from school, I was so happy for seeing her, for being with her, and I felt as if I hadn't seen her in a long time. I held her in my arms and kissed her forehead, and then we went to the Co-op on Earlsdon Street because she wanted something to eat, and from there we made our way to Poplar Road where I had parked my car and Leaf told me about her day at school and about a few games she had played on the previous night, and afterwards we returned to a conversation we had two days ago, something about Roblox and about a gamer who was wrongly banned from a game even though, according to my daughter's words, this gamer was wrongly accused of bullying another gamer; the gamer who got banned was actually a victim himself, not of bullying but of wrongly being accused of something he didn't do, and my daughter said that the soon-to-be-banned gamer tried in vain to protest his innocence and even pointed the finger at the guilty party but for whatever reason the guilty party managed to get away with his crime and no one else came to the innocent gamer's rescue, no one else apart from my daughter who also, by the sound of things, tried in vain to get the guilty gamer banned from the game instead of the innocent gamer. But it was too late and the innocent gamer got thrown out of the game by the creator of the game. And my daughter quit the game in protest.

I was making my way to Yu's place, driving us there, listening to a compilation CD I had made on that same morning. Benjamin Orr's *Stay The Night* was playing and it was followed by another track by Orr called *Even Angels Fall,* a beautiful track that was never released. I was listening to the music and listening to Leaf's story, and I said to her, "You should write this down; everything that happened, your side of the story, what you know, what you saw, the names of every single player involved. Start a journal and write it all down."

She nodded a couple of times before saying yeah, but I kind of knew she wouldn't write it down, not yet, not that week, maybe not even that year, not unless I told her again later on; not much later so she wouldn't forget the names of those involved, and apart from that I didn't say much at all. My job was to listen, occasionally nod, agree with what my daughter was saying, even smile, as I sat in the car, and because there were some works being done on the roads the traffic moved at a snail's speed and Leaf could finish the story.

After I dropped her home I waited for a bit longer outside, inside my car, so that I could see my son too. In those brief minutes while I waited for my son to arrive from school I became a child, too, almost an orphan, and I saw myself as a child living in Portugal, watching my friends with their parents, listening to them as they told me about their summer holidays and their Christmases parties with their parents and other members of the family, but me and my brother Carlos never had summer holidays or Christmases parties with our parents because our parents were absent for most of our lives, and when we finally saw our parents they had other families, other children, and Carlos and I were adults, too old to be children, to be treated as such, but that's life, or one of life's many faces, one of life's toughest chapters, and not only had I missed all of my Christmases with my parents (actually, now that I remember, I did spend one Christmas with my mum), now I was also missing Christmases with my children.

I sat in the car reading a collection of short stories by Eduardo Halfon, occasionally looking up, looking back, and a few minutes passed before Matthew arrived. He saw my car straight away and walked over to where I was, and I stepped out of the car the moment I saw him, the two of us slowly made our way towards one another, and then we hugged and I kissed his head and asked him how his day had been. No one could see how the divorced father, lonely writer, was suffering. No one could see the invisible tears I cried almost every single day but my journey through the darkness was slowly coming to an end; I could feel it, and then the roles would reverse and many of those who had caused me to cry would feel the pain themselves. It's the law of the universe, karma, call it whatever you want.

I spoke with my son for a few minutes and then he went home and I drove somewhere, nowhere really, I kid you not, and I parked my car somewhere, an unknown street, and instead of going home to rest for a couple of hours before my shift was about to start I stayed in the car, eyes closed, the alarm on my mobile phone set for later, and while I sat in the car I thought about the story that my daughter had told me, the story about the Roblox gamer who has wrongly accused of bullying other players and because of someone's lies he got banned from the game, and I wondered how that player felt when he got banned from the game; was he angry, was he sad, did he felt as if the world was a place of injustice, a place where truth didn't really matter, and would something like that influence his way of thinking, even of being around others? And then I thought about Ellie and about Yu, and about my brother Carlos and about so many people who were so jealous of me when I had a bit of happiness in my life, and I knew I was changing, not becoming colder but more cautious, and bit by bit I was leaving a lot of people behind, including family members, and I no longer bothered to keep in touch with a lot of people, which was fine by me; in fact it was a bit of a relief. I was in isolation, slowly leaving all that didn't matter behind. I was on the way out, moving towards another life. Unfortunately (but fortunately for me) I would have to leave a lot of people behind. There was no place for them in my new life but I was fine with it. The changes were already happening within me and I felt the urge to move somewhere else, start again, remain in God and start a new life. Some people's energies felt a bit off and I no longer wanted them around me. I was actually surprised by how I was feeling and by how much I was changing, but I sure needed to change.

I stayed nowhere for close to two hours, had a short nap, and then I drove to work, Coldplay's *Magic* playing loudly on my stereo. I was heading to work and at the same time I was heading somewhere completely new. Not then but soon. I smiled then. That story was coming to an end. It had been a long story. It started in 2019 and wasn't yet over but a new chapter (and a New Life) was calling out for me. I would have to embrace it and leave the Old Life behind, including past loves. Some faces from the past would one day become strangers and past loves would soon be forgotten. One day those same faces would wonder, "What happened to M÷? Why did he leave us?" but the truth is I didn't leave them. They were the ones who left me; some of them even abused me with their lies and coldness and selfishness, and that's why I had to erase them out of my life. Maybe I would return to them (and this story) later on, much later, but right then I just wanted to leave them behind for a long time, maybe even forever. And so I drove, not towards work but towards a New Life.

Madonna's *The Power of Goodbye* started to play. It was almost as if Madonna knew how I felt, almost as if she had written the song for me. What a track. Yes, it definitely was time to say goodbye to some people.

÷

I enter the City Arms, order a cup of coffee, think about ordering a cheese and egg muffin but after a few seconds decide that a cup of coffee is enough, and then I make my way to the coffee machine when I see the bisexual poet waving at me. She's actually waving a book in the air, a copy of my novel *cast away your dreams of darkness*, and after I get a decaffeinated coffee for me I join her and see that she has two other books with her. The books are *Lost Property* by Laura Beatty and *Making a Scene* by Constance Wu. There aren't that many people at the City Arms. Two men sitting alone eating large breakfasts, and two women sitting at the same table, facing one another, drinking coffee only. The machines are watching us from the inside of our mobile phones, watching us and recording our lives, seeing what we like, what we need, what we're addicted to, so that later on they can tempt us with more offerings. This is what I'm thinking about as I sit there listening to the poet, listening to her moan about her lack of ideas, about her parents who still don't know about her sexual preferences, listening to her moan about our government, China, Russia, the universe, and while she moans and complains the machines laugh at us. And then, because I'm a crazy writer (but, in my defence, most writers are a bit out there), I wonder if there are any Naga Lokas in the room, or even some sort of invisible aliens watching us right now, sitting really close to us, recording our talk so that later on he or she or whatever aliens are can download it and post it on some sort of alien YouTube channel so that the aliens can watch human life. My thoughts are so crazy that I feel like laughing but maybe this is no laughing matter.

And when the poet says, "I don't know what to write," I reply, "Neither do I."

But I do.

And the eight foot long white serpent floats in space, waiting for the next astronaut to arrive.

Epilogue

M÷ had nothing else to write. Not then.

The world was losing its soul but what could he do about it apart from waiting?

A few days ago, when he was in Tile Hill, he saw a man looking at the holes on the street, the holes on the road, massive holes that looked as if they were spreading throughout the city.

The man saw M÷ looking at him and said, "Nature is making a return. Mother Earth wants to go back to its natural habitat. We were given the world but we're destroying it and now Mother Earth wants us out. Or maybe the Creator wants us out.

"There will be no Flood. He told us in the Bible that there wouldn't be another flood, didn't He? I can't remember. Instead of the Flood Death will take another shape. Death will come from above. Fire."

M÷ didn't know what to say. He was a character in a movie, the longest movie of all time, a movie that had movies playing inside it. He wasn't even surprised that Steven Seagal was teaching martial arts to Russian troops. After all hadn't Ronald Reagan once upon a time been President of the United States? And Donald Trump, too? Even Arnold Schwarzenegger had been Governor of California.

M÷ nodded and went his way.

Meanwhile the Time Traveller was stuck in the loop, travelling everywhere, trying to avoid Death. Or maybe he was immortal, too.

The Machine was watching M÷.

In fact the Machine was watching them all.

There was no way of escaping the Machine. It was everywhere, even in the sky, in space, watching them, pushing for the end of the human race. And the end was slowly approaching. Or maybe not. Maybe M÷ would write another book. But not yet.

M÷ got in his car and drove to church. The roads were quiet at that time of the morning. Icehouse's *Taking the Town* was playing on his car radio. For the last few weeks M÷ had been listening to every single album of Icehouse, including the one that they had released as Flowers. He parked his car on Kingsland Avenue. Before going inside the church he grabbed a plastic bag with all his crystals and dropped the bag in a bin. He had the Rosary beads with him. That's all he needed.

He entered the church and kept on walking. The past was slowly being left behind. There was no one waiting for him, no one looking for him. Not yet. Not then.

Sometimes you have to leave people behind so that they know your worth.

M÷

Coventry, May 2023

FICTION FROM APS BOOKS

(www.andrewsparke.com)

AJ Woolfenden: *Mystique: A Bitten Past*
Alex O'Connor: *Time For The Polka Dot*
Alison Manning: *World Without Endless Sheep*
Andrew Sparke: *Abuse Cocaine & Soft Furnishings*
Andrew Sparke: *Copper Trance & Motorways*
Chris Grayling: *A Week Is…A Long Time*
Colin Mardell: *Fetch Them Home*
Colin Mardell: *Keep Her Safe*
Davey J Ashfield *Contracting With The Devil*
Davey J Ashfield: *A Turkey And One More Easter Egg*
Davey J Ashfield: *Footsteps On The Teign*
Des Tong *In Flames*
Des Tong: *Whatever It Takes Babe*
Fenella Bass: *Darkness*
Fenella Bass: *Hornbeams*
Fenella Bass:: *Shadows*
HR Beasley: *Nothing Left To Hide*
Hugh Lupus *An Extra Knot (Parts I-VIIII*
Hugh Lupus: *Mr. Donaldson's Company*
Ian Meacheam & Mark Peckett: *Seven Stages*
Ian Meacheam: *An Inspector Called*
Ian Meacheam: *Broad Lines Narrow Margins*
Ian Meacheam: *Time And The Consequences*
J.W.Darcy *Looking For Luca*
J.W.Darcy: *Ladybird Ladybird*
J.W.Darcy: *Legacy Of Lies*
J.W.Darcy: *Love Lust & Needful Things*
Jane Evans: *The Third Bridge*
Jean Harvey: *Pandemic*
Laurie Hornsby: *Postcards From The Seaside*
Lee Benson: *No Naked Walls*
Lee Benson: *Now You're The Artist…Deal With It*
Lee Benson: *So You Want To Own An Art Gallery*
Lee Benson: *Where's Your Art gallery Now?*
Lorna MacDonald-Bradley: *Dealga*
Mark Peckett: *Joffie's Mark*
Martin White: *Life Unfinished*
Michel Henri: *Abducted By Faerie*
Michel Henri: *Mister Penny Whistle*

Michel Henri: *The Death Of The Duchess Of Grasmere*
Milton Godfrey: *The Danger Lies In Fear*
Nargis Darby: *A Different Shade Of Love*
Paul C. Walsh: *A Place Between The Mountains*
Paul C. Walsh: *Hallowed Turf*
Paul Dickinson: *Franzi The Hero*
Peter Georgiadis: *Not Cast In Stone*
Peter Georgiadis: *The Mute Swan's Song*
Peter Georgiadis: *The Murderous Journey*
Peter Raposo: *All Women Are Mortal*
Peter Raposo: *cast away your dreams of darkness*
Peter Raposo: *dUst*
Peter Raposo: *Pussy Foot*
Peter Raposo: *Second Life*
Peter Raposo: *Talk About Proust*
Peter Raposo: *the illusion of movement*
Peter Raposo: *The Sinking City*
Peter Raposo: *This Is Not The End*
Peter Raposo: *those who lie will fade and die*
Phil Thompson: *Momentary Lapses In Concentration*
Simon Falshaw: *The Stone*
TF Byrne *Damage Limitation*
Tony Rowland: *Traitor Lodger German Spy*
Tony Saunders: *Publish and Be Dead*
Various: *Brumology*
Various: *Unshriven*

APS PUBLICATIONS

Printed in Poland
by Amazon Fulfillment
Poland Sp. z o.o., Wrocław
18 June 2023

57d4a527-66f6-40a4-a5e2-521c0025ffc9R01